SHATTERED

Copyright © 2022 by Natalia Lourose

All rights reserved.

No part of this book may be reproduced in any form or by any electronic or mechanical means, including information storage and retrieval systems, without written permission from the author, except for the use of brief quotations in a book review.

Editor: Makenzie @ Nice Girl, Naughty Edits

❦ Created with Vellum

SHATTERED

A DARK ROMANCE

NATALIA LOUROSE

PLAYLIST

Numb - Carlie Hanson
Haunting - Halsey
Monsters - All Time Low
Jerk - Oliver Tree
Into the Dark - Bring Me the Horizon
Time - NF
The Fire - Bishop Briggs
Waste Love - Machine Gun Kelly
Tonight is the Night I die, Palaye Royale
Blood//Water - Grandson
Let You Down - NF
Despicable - Grandson
When the Truth Hunts You Down - Sam Tinnesz

Listen to the Full Playlist on Spotify

To my sister,
Thank you for being so supportive of my dreams. Everyone
deserves someone like you in their life.
But please don't reads this book.

Only a fool accepts the evidence of his own memory as gospel. And we're all fools.

MALCOLM GLADWELL

CONTENT WARNING

This is not a guide to relationships. This is a dark romance with several aspects that could be considered triggering. I urge you to read the below content warning or review to be sure that this content is safe for you. Your mental health comes first.

Triggering content includes: homicide, drugs, sexual assault, coercion, mental health disorders, and abuse.

Shattered also contains graphic sexual content with scenes including: spanking/punishment, rope/ties, group scene, and choking.

1

mik

I'm barely awake when they come for me. Sleep doesn't reach me easily anymore. I toss and turn at night, images of my sister flashing through my head like a fucked up slide show. I see her everywhere, her mangled corpse haunting me. The aftermath of my restless night has left me limp and tired, my eyes still puffy from my midnight cry. But I don't have time to calm the swelling before the door to my dorm room is swung open.

I don't need words to know why they're here. I always expected him to send someone for me. He's not very good at not getting what he wants, and right now he wants me regardless of whether or not I want him. The two men stand in the entrance to my bedroom like they own the place, and in some way, maybe they do. Vaughn's family donates a lot of money to my small state college. He could set a building on fire and the staff would smile and wave, not one would bat an eye.

They dwarf the place, with Vaughn hovering over my dresser, his thick fingers tracing the lines of my picture frames. Me and Auden at the beach, me and Auden in the backyard of our old house. I wince. Their tall and lean bodies make my dorm room feel small and crowded. I always feel small around them.

"It's time, Mik," Vaughn says. Strong arms cross his body as he stands at the edge of my bed. He's intimidating, the way his muscles contract and his dark eyes watch me. Power drips from his stance, the dominating gesture shouting, *listen to me, or else.*

I choose to listen. My light blue blanket falls from my body when I stand, exposing my pale, bare legs to them. I tug at the hem of the oversized sleep shirt, attempting the smallest amount of modesty and failing.

I'm glad that it's just the two of them, a small miracle. There should be four, but Noah and Pax are missing. Half of the pack is much more manageable. Beckett stands behind Vaughn, leaning his own large body against the frame of the door. I'm thankful for his presence; he was always the nicest.

"Can I pack a bag?" I ask sheepishly. I'm surprised I wasn't already hauled over a shoulder and dragged from my room kicking and screaming, so even though my heart is clenched and my stomach is threatening to betray me, I feel just the smallest amount of gratitude.

"Quickly," Vaughn spits.

"Shower?" I try. Why stop when I'm ahead?

Beckett rolls his eyes, but it's Vaughn who answers me. "Not enough time, Mikaela."

I nod solemnly and head to my dresser. I pull a pair of skinny jeans up my legs, a feeble attempt to hide some skin from them, but it's not that they haven't seen it before. They've seen every inch of my body, felt my skin, heard me moan... and now I feel their eyes watching me as I grab a duffle bag from my closet and throw clothes from my dresser into it.

Footsteps thud behind me, and a glance over my shoulder shows Beckett pacing through the small room. He jabs a finger at a framed needlepoint reading: *be someone who makes you happy.* "What's with all the quotes?" he asks, a single brow lifting in amusement.

"My mom," I mutter. Beckett only laughs and moves on from the needlepoint to the corkboard filled with inspirational quotes printed out on paper and secured to the board with thumbtacks.

Every cliché you could think of are pinned there.

You got this, girl.

She believed she could, so she did.

You are a strong, independent woman.

My mother has scattered the quotes all throughout my dorm room. Little sayings she finds online and prints out with an old inkjet printer. When that wasn't enough, she started to cross stitch quotes and then framed the finished products. She hangs them on the walls, sets the frames up on bare surfaces, pins a quote to the fridge with a magnet. She fills the blank spaces of my room with her little bits of positivity.

When I see Vaughn and Beckett next to the pretty words, all I can imagine is *him.* The bad memories flood my mind and I try to read one of the positive words saying, *you can do anything,* but they blend with the fear, and the pain wins every time.

I can't blame my mom for trying, for making every attempt to make my world better, brighter.

She's doing anything she can to keep me hanging on.

My mother is a firm believer that what you think becomes your reality. She lives in the world of *The Secret* and tries her hardest to drag me along with her.

But she doesn't know these men the way I do.

She thinks there's a war to be won here, that the truth

always comes out in the end, but she doesn't know. She doesn't know this family like I do.

"Let's go," Vaughn demands.

I take one last glance at myself. Dark, oversized hoodie, tight jeans, no makeup. My hair was wet when I went to sleep, so now it hangs in messy, unbrushed waves.

He's not going to like what he sees.

Maybe he'll let me go, then.

It's a silly thought though, because Noah Bancroft will never let me go.

2

Halloween Night, One Year Earlier

My mother's face lights up when my sister descends the stairs, her hair twisted back in a low bun with loose tendrils curled at the front. She looks like the golden child that she is. Mom casts me a sideways glance as I crunch on a potato chip, sitting on the sofa with my feet kicked up on the coffee table.

When it was my chance to go to prom, I didn't, effectively ruining my mother's fantasy of seeing me in a frilly gown. She jumped at the chance to buy Auden a fancy dress, even if only for a Halloween costume.

That's the difference between Auden and me.

She's the good child. She plays soccer, gets straight As, and wears the cutest dresses my mother fawns over. I smoke too much and barely got into college. In my mother's eyes, the only success I've had is getting Noah Bancroft to fall in love with me. Dating the town's golden boy is an A+ for her.

"You look beautiful," Mom gushes, placing each of her hands on Auden's shoulders in that loving way that mothers do.

Auden's lips, covered in pink gloss, tug up into a smile. She really does look beautiful, a fact that even I can't deny. Yet I can't quite place where my annoyance at my little sister is coming from.

It could be the fact that she's living the ultimate high school experience, the one they show in movies, the one you're supposed to want. Athlete, honor roll, popularity.

Or it could be the way my mother looks at her with love and amazement, like she could do no wrong. It brings a pang to my stomach, makes me feel sick. My mother loves me, I think I know that. But it's different with Auden.

Mom poses Auden on the stairway, fluffing her dress and snapping far too many pictures. After each click of the shutter, she leans back from the camera and admires her youngest daughter for another moment.

She doesn't look at me that way.

My bare feet drop from the coffee table with a thud, and grabbing the empty bag of chips, I head to the kitchen. Crumpling the garbage and throwing it into the can, I take a deep breath, clearing out my head.

My therapist would tell me to breathe through it, to remember all the good things in my life. My family is normal. We have a home, cars, and food on the table. I count my blessings, remind myself that I'm okay.

Inhale.

Exhale.

I'm *okay*.

What she forgets is that my anxiety doesn't see things the way *normal* people do. I have a good life, but I cling to the bad, to the hopeless. I let myself spiral in situations that have never happened. I cling to the what-ifs. Forcing myself to live in an anxiety filled world that only exists within the walls of my mind.

"What are you up to tonight, champ?" I cringe at the nickname my father uses. Judah Wilder comes into the kitchen at 8 PM, dropping his briefcase on the table and patting me on the shoulder. He's home late, which is his normal routine since we moved here.

I think he really wanted boys, since he doesn't know how to adjust to only having women in the house. For twenty years, he's called me *champ*. A silly nickname considering I've never won anything in my whole life and definitely not a sport.

"Party at Noah's," I tell him, spinning on my heel to face him as he pulls off his blazer, tossing it over the back of a chair and loosening his tie. He's quick to lose everything that puts him in work mode when he gets home. It's like he needs to rid himself of the office. I think he feels dirty working there, but the pay is too much to pass up, so he dons the suit and tie and puts on a brave face.

My father was an artist before mom got pregnant with me. Now he's just a dad and lobbies for things he doesn't care about, which includes working for one of the richest men in the country. He tries to keep the two separate, but with the long hours, the two things have begun to bleed together.

"Bad day?" I ask.

Wrinkles line his eyes as he tries to answer me with a lie. "Nah." He shrugs. "Don't worry about it." He walks back over to me, pressing a kiss to my forehead. "Noah's good to you?" he asks, narrowing his eyes and changing the subject. He doesn't want to talk about work, the people he works for, or the things he does. It's soul sucking for him, I can tell.

I snort a laugh. "Yeah, Dad, he's good."

If he wasn't, Dad wouldn't do a damn thing about it. Not that he wouldn't want to, but he can't. Noah's dad is his boss.

"Good." He pulls away, peeking into the living room where mom is still taking pictures of Auden in her princess costume. What seventeen-year-old dresses up as a princess for Halloween anyway?

He chuckles when he sees her, then stalks to the fridge to grab a beer. He's been drinking more since we moved to Aspen Falls two years ago for this job. Before that, we lived in North Carolina where he still worked a mind-numbing job, just one that got him home on time for dinner.

I don't say anything as he cracks the top and takes a chug from the can.

"You driving Auden to her party?"

"Unfortunately," I mumble.

"Hey"—he comes closer to me again, resting a hand on my shoulder—"you know, I used to hate my brother. We were always on each other's cases—"

"And now you're best friends," I cut him off with a smile. "I know, Dad. You tell me this story all the time."

He grins. "And it's still true. One day, you'll regret that you weren't close when you were young. Don't push her away."

He presses another kiss to my forehead, and then leaves me standing there in the kitchen, waiting on my little sister.

Present

No words are spoken as we ride from the city into the suburbs. Vaughn races his Range Rover down the highway and Beckett drums his fingertips against the passenger side door, the rhythm matching that of my anxiety. A steady drum in my heart telling me this is a bad idea.

These men are not my friends.

At least… not anymore.

"Where is he?" I ask as we pass the high school, a pang of grief strikes my chest when I remember the times I dropped Auden off at that door. My heart beats heavily in my chest, and I rub my clammy hands along the rough surface of my jeans. A memory of the last time I saw Noah is lingering in my mind, his anger rolling off in waves. He doesn't like what my family did to him… and I don't like what he did to us. I guess that means we're in some kind of stalemate. A wicked game of who makes the next move.

I guess it's him.

Beckett turns to face me with a grin. "You worried?" he asks.

"No." I try to shake it off, willing my fingers to stop sweating, for my leg to stay still. The anxiety is palpable. It's clear to everyone in this car that Noah has me shaken up and I haven't even seen him yet.

"Ah, Mik." I catch his eyes in the rearview mirror before his head turns and I can see the ever-growing smirk lining his lips. Vaughn chuckles from the front seat as Beckett reaches into the back to pat my knee condescendingly. "Don't worry, little girl," he coos. "You're safe." He turns back to the front. "For now," he adds over his shoulder.

I shudder.

My mom asks me every day why I'm moody.

Why I need a bottle of Xanax to go along with my antidepressants?

Why my nightmares pull me from sleep every night?

These guys.

Noah. Vaughn. Beckett. Pax.

That night.

There's an emptiness that swirls around in my mind, and at the edges I see them, all four of them. I don't have the words or memories to place them there, at the scene of the crime, but I know they were.

But feelings don't count for anything. The only way to get a conviction is with evidence, and there's none of that.

Noah is waiting when we arrive at his house. A huge home tucked away in a private development filled with other rich assholes. Each of the guys has a house here, each designed specifically for them.

Noah's is newer, a pristine prison of his creation. The development is made to look classy, sprawled out over multiple acres of land, leaving plenty of room between each house. Enough that my screams will be drowned out. Not that it matters anyway, no one is going to call the cops on a Bancroft.

No one except... me, maybe.

Noah is leaning against the brown leather couch, ankles crossed, the sleeves of his white dress shirt rolled to his elbows, exposing his strong tattooed forearms.

"Mik," he says calmly. There's not a flicker of emotion for me to grasp on to. His face is eerily put together, voice controlled. Then again, Noah doesn't lose control in front of others, only behind closed doors.

My voice doesn't work. I feel betrayed by my body. Instead of greeting him, I stand in the doorway, staring.

Beckett chuckles, tossing my duffle bag on the couch before unzipping it and removing the contents. "What are you doing?" I ask, my voice finally coming back to me. As long as I'm not talking to *him*, I'm fine.

Vaughn closes the front door to Noah's home, locking it

behind us before joining Beckett. They're emptying the bag and checking all the contents. Holding up shirts and shaking them out, digging through my makeup. They check it all.

They probably think I brought a bug with me. A camera, a recorder, something that would make Noah's situation worse. They're protective of him; he's like a brother to them and they won't take a chance that I would be able to betray him, again.

"Upstairs," Noah says next, and immediately he turns to the stairway and starts to climb the steps, expecting me to follow.

Knowing this was coming, I rehearsed what I would say to him every night in my head, but now that the moment is here, my mind lies completely blank. I can't find the words to tell him to fuck off, to leave me alone. I have so many other things I want to say, questions I want to ask. I don't trust him to tell me the truth. Not now. Maybe not ever.

"Now, Mik," he snarls.

I follow him. My legs carry me up the stairs, even though my heart is unwilling. My head, on the other hand, knows I don't have a choice. Beckett and Vaughn are watching me as I go. I can practically feel Vaughn's grin searing into my back. He's enjoying my pain too much.

"We're not teenagers anymore. You can't boss me around to impress your friends," I spit out as soon as he closes his bedroom door behind me.

His room is large, filled with dark furniture and fabrics. The only source of light comes from the large window facing the secluded street. It feels sophisticated here, too mature for a twenty-something. But Noah has been preparing to be an adult his entire life. Now, at twenty-five, he has the house of a fifty-year-old businessman.

He quirks an eyebrow, amused by my outburst, but he doesn't say anything. His eyes crawl up and down my body, making goosebumps rise across my flesh. I feel naked under his gaze, like he can see through the layers of clothing, through the invisible brick wall I've built to guard my heart.

I press my back against the door, feeling small under his gaze. I always have, from the moment I laid eyes on Noah. I felt beneath him.

"You can't just kidnap me." I add.

"No?" He's trying to control the smirk that threatens to rise on his lips. He's always in control. Every emotion is under strict regulation. Unlike me, I wear my heart on my sleeve. Every emotion is written across my face sooner than I can articulate the thought.

"No," I state. "I'm not yours."

He hums thoughtfully, nodding. Grabbing the tie off the top of his dresser, he strings it through the collar of his dress shirt and ties the knot slowly.

He's toying with me, I know this. Still, a sweat breaks out across my skin, and I shift from side to side as my stomach churns.

I know what he's capable of.

But I don't know what he's going to do to me.

"Are you done now?" he finally asks me, after the panic has taken control of my body. I nod, my vocal cords no longer wanting to work.

"Good, because here's the thing, Mik." He stalks closer to me, pressing his body against mine. He takes over my space, filling all my senses with him. His scent, black coffee and cedarwood, fills my nostrils. Brown eyes peer into mine, his warm body covering me. "You are mine. You've always been mine. You will always be mine. Mine to hold, mine to hurt, mine to love. Do you get that yet, baby?" he whispers the last sentence in my ear, sending a chill down my neck.

"Yours to kill?" The words come out in a whisper. I don't know why I say it, but before I can think better of it, I do. I know he could. If he wanted to, Noah could have me gone in minutes. By his hand or his orders, it wouldn't matter much. There's a part of me that thinks he's keeping me alive simply to avoid the press my death might bring. But there's another part, a girlish dream that thinks Noah would *never* hurt me.

He chuckles, bringing his head back just enough for me to take in his face again. Strong, clean-shaven jawline, high cheekbones, deep brown eyes. "Yeah, baby, if I want to. But lucky for you, I don't." He pushes off the door and backs away from me.

I inhale a breath like I've never breathed before, letting the fresh air fill my lungs and calm my nerves. I can't think when he's that close to me, when his scent is lingering in my nose, overtaking all my senses.

"Get dressed," he tells me as he heads to his closet.

"For what?"

Noah tosses me an annoyed look over his shoulder. "We're making a statement today."

I feel cold, like the blood has stopped moving through my body. I don't move, I only sink farther back against the door.

"Wear a nice dress," he tells me. "Do your hair, put on makeup, play your part, Mik."

"And if I don't?" I question.

"Don't test me." he gives me a stern look.

My chest feels tight. I don't have a lot of options right now. I'm lacking people who trust me, or even want me. If I run from him… he'll just find me again. "It's going to kill them."

Doing what he wants will break my family, more than he already has. If I don't do what he wants… my parents might lose their last daughter, and I don't know if they can take that either.

Neither option is a good one.

I rub a hand over my heart, hoping that the motion will soothe the ache rising in my chest. "I can't," I whisper, mostly to myself.

"You can, Mik." He's watching me through the mirror above his dresser while he finishes getting ready, dabbing cologne on his wrists, straightening his suit.

"Noah." His name comes out whiny. Maybe I am whiny. I'm desperate. "Please."

Dark eyes burn a hole into me when he spins to face me. He likes when I fight, but not about this. Noah wants me to listen to him, obey him, and I'm not doing that right now.

It's a choice he's giving me; making me choose between him and my family. Standing by his side will solidify that choice, and he knows it.

He picks up a small box from the dresser, rolling the thing in his palm while he thinks. When he does talk again, he's vicious. "Put on a pretty dress, do your makeup, and wear this fucking ring." He tosses the small black velvet box at me.

I don't catch it and it falls to the floor with a soft thud. His eyes darken as he stalks over to me. Plucking the box from the floor, he flips open the lid to reveal the ornate diamond on a gold diamond encrusted band. The thing is huge, bigger than what I would have wanted if he would have asked.

"Put it on," he growls, shoving the ring at me.

A sob lodges itself in my throat. "Don't make me." I'm pointlessly pleading now, with whatever shred of humanity he has left.

I loved this man in front of me at one time. Before, I think. Before, when it was easy. When being together was simple. Now, it's hard. The lies, the past, everything is harder now. When I look at Noah Bancroft, I only see danger.

For a while, it was clouded. The danger was hidden beneath so many layers, I mistook it for safety.

But I didn't know then what I know now.

I'm fisting my hands at my sides, the nails biting into my palms. I don't know if I'm more afraid that he'll force the ring on me or that I would willingly take it. He heaves a sigh, leaning forward and pressing his forehead against mine.

"Mik," he whispers, and for some reason, his deep voice is still comforting to me. I have to work to not let myself fall under his spell again, because being under his spell is beautiful and warm and safe. It's hard to separate the feelings of the past from the truth of the present. It's hard not to let myself sink back into him. "I'm sorry things are like this," he tells me. "You know I never want to hurt you."

Somewhere deep down, I think that's true. I alternate between thinking Noah's a monster and thinking there's a good person trapped inside that body.

"I need you," he breathes. Warm lips touch my forehead, the featherlight kisses giving me goosebumps.

I hate when he's sweet like this. It's a trick, but my body responds to him. Heat travels in an instant up my core from my low belly. My mind starts to switch tracks, starts to forget I'm in the presence of a villain.

His hands trace up the side of my body, my fists loosening as he grazes them. He leans down, kissing along my neck, under my chin.

"Noah—"

"Say yes." He kisses my cheek, my lips, my forehead. "Say yes, Mik," he whispers in my ear.

He lifts the ring up again, holding it in front of my face. No longer a threat, but a request.

Begrudgingly, I extend my left hand for him, letting him slip the ring onto my finger. He kisses it once it's there, then gives me a smug look.

"Get dressed," he says. "I'm not asking again."

3

Depression is a bitch. One that keeps me curled under my blankets, locked in my room for days on end. If my mother didn't bring me groceries and unpack them, I probably wouldn't eat.

I've become such a hermit, I've forgotten what having my hair and makeup done feels like. But the dress feels too tight, and the padded bra has a wire that's pressing into my skin. I would much rather be at home in sweats and a t-shirt.

Noah wraps an arm around my waist in a dominating gesture while he talks to his lawyer in a hushed whisper. News vans have already begun to arrive. Reporters and cameras fill the front steps of the courthouse.

There's a sick feeling swishing around in my stomach. I should run, I think, but my feet stay glued to the cement. And besides, the pointed heels Noah handed me aren't made for running. No, these are made for captivity, keeping me pretty and close to him.

It seems Noah had everything planned and prepared. A modest black long-sleeved dress and a pair of matching black heels were laid out for me, picked out by his personal shopper. I put on some light makeup while he watched over my shoulder. I didn't curl my hair to his dismay, instead I ran my fingers through the dirty blonde waves and scrunched them with some of his gel.

I'm not model pretty. I don't look worthy of being Noah Bancroft's wife, but I look better than I have in a while. Noah still appreciates my looks, though. After I was dressed and ready, he cupped a warm hand over my cheek, tracing his thumb along my freckles. I saw the smallest hint of a smile, and I wondered how long it'd been since he did. Since he was happy. Butterflies swarmed my insides at seeing that smile, bouncing off my ribs.

But then I remembered the hate I have for him/boiling in my stomach.

I'm not listening to the conversation happening between Noah and his lawyer until I feel his hand flex on my waist, tightening his grip. My eyes dart from the news vans up to my fiancé. He doesn't look angry when his eyes meet mine, and he ducks his head down so he can whisper in my ear.

"Are you listening?"

I shake my head no. He nods to the lawyer.

The guy is probably ten years our senior, looking sharp in his fitted suit and shiny shoes. His hair slicked back, he's tall and handsome. For a minute, I wonder what he's like behind closed doors. Is he an asshole or is he nice?

"Mikaela." He looks at me with annoyance at having to repeat himself. "I want you to stand close to Noah, look like the happy couple who just suffered a loss."

I snort, the sound of my laugh making both men scowl at me.

"You think people are going to believe this façade?" I ask, a slight attitude to my voice.

His lawyer grimaces at me and then turns back to Noah.

"I thought you said you two were good?" He looks worried.

I feel a grin spread on my face, a smug satisfaction that he caught Noah in a lie.

Noah's grip tightens around my waist again; a silent warning to behave. "We are," he tells the lawyer. The guy sighs heavily, his hands hitting his hips, eyes looking out to the crowd that has gathered.

It's a lot of people.

Mostly reporters. The case has drawn both local and national news.

A billionaire's son on trial for murder is a big story.

Noah's parents arrive next. His mother, Mariam, wears a black pencil skirt with a matching silk top. Her blonde hair is twisted back elegantly, and she's wearing huge diamond earrings that match the ring on her finger. She looks chic and sophisticated. A proper wife, something I will never be.

Beside her is Noah's father, Edward, a tall and thickly built man sporting a navy-blue suit. His salt and pepper hair is slicked back and matches the trimmed beard on his face. He wraps an arm around his wife as they stop in front of us. His gaze lands on Noah, and they share a look.

I imagine they're silently communicating, a secret language made of quick eye contact and nods. Edward asking if I'm going to cooperate and Noah telling him yes. Even though he doesn't know that for sure.

The lawyer speaks first, addressing the media and crowd and introducing Noah, not that he needs an introduction.

Everyone in Aspen Hill knows him.

The resident pretty boy, son of the town's richest man.

The man whose company employs half of this town.

"Good afternoon, everyone," Noah begins his statement. My fingers interlace in front of me as I stand at his side while he speaks. I want to drone him out, want to look away, but I can't. I need to hear what he says.

I need to know why he thinks he's innocent.

"I would like to extend my deepest sympathy to the family of Auden Wilder." He looks over at me. "Including my fiancée, Mikaela, Auden's sister."

My chest tightens, and I regret coming with him. Not that he gave me much of a choice. I feel like my legs might buckle if I stand here any longer, but I'm frozen, caught in his warm gaze.

He looks different talking to these people. Sadder, warmer, more compassionate.

He definitely doesn't look like a killer.

"Auden was deeply loved by this community," he continues, "and also by my family. Our world has been turned upside down in the wake of her devastating death, not only because we miss her, but because of these false accusations."

I focus on my breathing.

In.

Out.

In.

Out.

"I'm looking forward to proving my innocence in court. It is time to put this all behind us so my family and I, especially Mikaela, can return to mourning Auden's death in private."

I don't know that I'm crying until Noah wipes a tear away. He's gentle in a way that surprises me, reaching over and placing a light palm on my cheek, using the other hand to softly brush away the stray tear.

The gesture reminds me of easier times, before everything got so hard. I want to lean into his palm, let the warmth of his skin comfort me. Give up, let Noah take care of me.

Then I remember we're still in front of the press, putting on a show. The cameras are facing us and if there's one thing Noah cares about, it's his public perception. I pull my face out of his grip and avert my gaze. Instead, zoning back into his lawyer, who is back at the microphone, announcing his crusade.

Noah Bancroft will not be convicted.

NOAH HAS AN ANKLE MONITOR, a condition of his bail.

One that honestly made me feel safer. But now that I'm back in his clutches, it means I'm also under house arrest alongside him. Not that the mansion he lives in is really a hardship, it's just the company I'm keeping at the moment that bothers me.

The place is spacious, way bigger than the three-bedroom home my family lives in. And every room here is at least three times the size of my dorm.

Since the statement, Noah has been locked in a room downstairs with his father and lawyer. Mariam fiddles in the kitchen, probably leaving too much food for us, which is fine by me because I have no intention of cooking for Noah.

I ditched the black dress as soon as we got back, instead wearing a pair of black leggings and an oversized sweatshirt long enough to cover my ass and the tops of my thighs.

Once I pull my hair into a ponytail, I wipe off the makeup, then slip my feet into a pair of warm socks. Noah had all my things brought into his room while we were gone, but I don't want them in there.

I check the hallway to make sure no one is around and then slip out of his bedroom. He told me to stay, commanding me like a dog when he brought me up here after the statement.

I'm not really well behaved.

This house is new to me. A shiny new, gold-plated cage he bought to serve his house arrest in. I check every door in the hallway. I find the bathroom, a linen closet, and finally a spare room. It looks well kept, clean, and unused.

It's a risk to deny him. A constant battle of wondering if he'll find it cute or sinful.

The latter will most likely earn me a punishment.

I head back to Noah's room to pack my things and move down the hall. There's not much here that's mine since I only packed a small bag. I fill it back up with my belongings. Ripping my clothing from the closet, makeup from the dresser, everything of mine I can find. It only takes me two trips.

I shove all my items into drawers and the closet, not really caring how organized the room is. I'm not looking for perfection, I just want space. I need to be away from him to breathe, to think, to grieve. The further the better, but I'll take what I can get.

When I'm done, I venture back out into the hallway, still needing to explore the rest of the house. I walk lightly, avoiding making a sound. I don't think I've been so quiet my entire life. The grand staircase leads downstairs to an open living and dining area. The back wall boasts a huge fireplace with tall windows looking out to the backyard and the forest behind it.

The place is cozy, decorated with dark woods, leather, and shades of blue. Noah can't match to save his life, so I know he hired someone to decorate. It's like dropping pennies for Noah to hire someone to do the things he doesn't want to. Decorators, chefs, even someone to buy him clothes.

The house is perfect. It's the type of home I would have dreamed about when we were together. The type of place I hoped we'd grow old in. Even now, I can picture it. The future we'll never have. The two of us, sitting in wooden rocking chairs while we watch the sun set.

I wander to the windows, looking out to the backyard covered in leaves. The trees of the forest are no longer green, now in shades of yellow, orange, and red. Leaves drop from them, fluttering to the ground. It's a stunning view. For a moment I grieve what almost was. The future he took away from me.

"Do you want something? Coffee?"

The voice startles me, and I jump before spinning quickly to face Mariam.

"Sorry." Her red painted lips turn into a sympathetic smile. "I didn't mean to scare you."

"It's okay." I wrap my arms around myself, suddenly cold as I face the mother of my sister's killer. I wonder if she knows what he's done. I wonder what she thinks of this whole charade. The morning after, did he tell her? Did he walk into his parents' bedroom and kneel next to their bed, confessing his crime to her?

There's a sympathetic look on her face and I have a hard time deciphering if she feels guilty or if she just feels bad for me.

Sympathy is something I've grown accustomed to. News of Auden's death spread like wildfire, and it wasn't long until people I'd never met could pick me out on the street. Fingers pointed, lingering stares—I was no longer average.

"So, do you want that coffee?" she asks again, a solemn tone in her voice. She probably doesn't know how to talk to me anymore. Should she be chipper, happy, sad? What emotion is right to talk to the girl with the dead sister?

I'm nervous to drink anything from her. Apprehensive to take anything from within these walls, really. I'm not sure what the endgame is. If that little stunt this morning doesn't work, will poisoning me be next?

Are two dead sisters better than one?

"No, thank you," I mutter.

Letting out a sigh, she places each of her hands on her waist. She's still wearing the black pencil skirt and silk top. She ditched the heels at some point, opting for walking around in stocking covered feet. Even so, she still looks perfect.

Perfect is practically the slogan of the Bancroft house. Everything there fits perfectly together. A happy family. A father who runs a Fortune 500 company, the perfect mother and wife who tends to the home and organizes charity events, and the son who's training to take over the company.

"Have you eaten anything today, Mikaela?" she asks.

I can't remember the last time I've eaten. Maybe yesterday? I think I had a slice of bread with peanut butter for dinner. The boys dragged me here this morning, and then the press conference, and now here I am. I don't even know what time it is, since Vaughn never gave me my phone back. I shake my head no.

She huffs. "Come on," she says, grabbing my arms and leading me to the kitchen. The room is massive and has more storage space than anyone would ever need. The base cabinets are a dark, moody shade of blue that contrasts nicely with floating wood shelves above them.

I take a seat at the island as Mariam fiddles around making some tea. She pours the hot water from the kettle over the tea bags she placed in each of our cups. "It's chai," she tells me. "I have a feeling you need something warm."

While the tea steeps, she sets off to find something to eat. She pulls out a loaf of fresh Italian bread and some deli meat from the fridge, setting everything up on the counter between us.

I let her make me a sandwich, even though I don't plan on touching it.

Mariam is nicer than Edward. For a while, I thought she was the reason behind all of the things I loved about Noah. He had a sweetness to him that matched hers.

He's not sweet, though.

He's cruel, calculated, a monster.

"How are you feeling?" she asks as she sets the sandwich in front of me.

"Fine." My voice comes out soft. Everything about me is soft lately. I'm quiet, reserved. I'm different from the woman I used to be. I don't think I even remember my old self.

I've divided my life into before and after. Before, when Auden was alive. When my parents were happy. When everything was right. And after it all went to hell.

I can pinpoint the exact moment that ruined everything, almost to the second.

It was meeting him.

I wish I would have never let Noah Bancroft into my life, into my *family's* life. I wish we would have never met. Maybe then Auden would still be here.

"It's okay if you're not," she tells me, sympathy dripping from her words.

I don't like people feeling sorry for me. I've worn the "girl with the dead sister" like a badge pinned to my chest for the past year, and even after all that time, I still can't stomach the sympathetic words and looks. The tiny bit of relief that comes from knowing something happened to me and not them.

Everyone feels bad for me.

I don't want pity. I want my sister back.

I leave Mariam in the kitchen, after barely touching my sandwich, and head back up to the room I claimed. Noah is still hidden in his office, having no use for me after I fulfilled my duty. He uses me when he needs me and discards me like a used object once he's done with me.

As I collapse back onto the bed, the memory foam mattress dips under my weight. Pulling the soft comforter up to my chin, I rest my eyes for a moment. I want to take comfort in being among these luxurious things. Before, I would have enjoyed them. I loved the wealth that came along with Noah; how easy everything suddenly was. Money opened doors that my family never had access to.

My family isn't poor. We're upper middle class, but nothing compared to having money like the Bancrofts. Billions of dollars just sitting in bank accounts. The kind of money that frees you from any consequences.

Being with him was electrifying. I felt on top of the world. He had fancy cars, beautiful clothes, and ate at the best restaurants. I felt like I was someone when I was with him.

His friends accepted me into their group as one of their own, and for the first time in my life, I felt like I belonged.

And then suddenly everything changed.

I lift my hand, glancing at the rock on my finger. He gave it to me that night, before everything went to shit.

A single night changed the course of everything. He had asked me to marry him, before Auden, before I got so drunk, I couldn't remember what happened. I went from the happiest moment of my life to the worst in a span of hours. Everything from that night is distorted, blurry. I remember the beginning but not the ending.

I huff, pulling the ring from my finger and tossing it onto the side table. I can't wear the damn thing more than I have to.

4

noah

Three Years Earlier

I'm staring at my reflection in the mirror, my fingers gripped around the edges of the marble countertop while I count the seconds of my breaths. In for four seconds, hold for four, out for four, hold for four. Repeat. *They teach this in the military.* At least that's what Laurel had told me. Laurel, the only one I can talk to about the sleepless nights, about the rage that lingers under my fingers. The itch I have to wrap around someone's throat and squeeze.

I'm thinking about my fucked up brain when Mikaela Wilder walks into the bathroom. She freezes, her bold green eyes meeting mine.

I recognize her from the picture on her dad's desk, one of those senior portraits where she's wearing a black shirt that exposes the tops of her shoulders. She doesn't actually look happy in the photo. Her pink lips are spread wide but there's no real smile there. It's forced. Just like mine. I think about that every time I see the picture. Not that often, but enough, when I have to go into his office for something or other.

Judah Wilder, her father, works for me. Or works for my father, I guess. Kind of the same thing at the end of the day. I wonder what that feels like for him, reporting to a kid not much older than his daughter, all because of nepotism. I laugh to myself, and Mikaela looks startled, confusion lining her features.

"I'm sorry," she mutters, her converse clad feet already backtracking, ready to leave the moment she intruded on.

"Why?" My question makes her pause and her eyes dart around, looking for a reason, an excuse. "I didn't lock the door," I say. "Why are you apologizing?"

Her lips press together in a thin line, but those green eyes are glued to mine. "I guess it's just a thing I do…" She trails off.

"You just go around apologizing for shit that's not your fault?" I laugh again and she wraps her arm around her midsection in a defensive gesture. She pulls her bottom lip between her teeth, gnawing on it while she thinks over her answer.

The older of the two Wilder girls has pale blonde hair that hangs in waves down to her breasts, with wispy bangs that are far too long. My fingers itch to push them to the side, tuck them behind her ears. I want to see her without the layer of protection they provide.

"No," she mutters, "Well, yeah. Maybe."

I can't help the way my lips tick up into a smile, nor the laughter that tumbles from them. She runs a hand through her blonde locks, brushing out the remnants of curls there.

"Do you smoke, Mikaela Wilder?"

The green disappears from her eyes as her pupils widen. "How do you-"

"Your picture is in your dad's office."

"You work with my dad?"

"Your dad works for me."

She pauses for a moment, those pretty pink lips pressing together while thoughts spiral through her mind. Mikaela wears her heart on her sleeve, her thoughts too. She's transparent, showing every emotion on the lines of her pale face.

"You're Noah, then."

"Yep." I grin, but she doesn't give me much of a smile back. "So," I prod, "do you smoke or not?"

"Smoke…?"

"Weed."

"I've never…"

"There's a first time for everything," I say. Those green eyes skim over me and I wonder if she's thinking about it. Or maybe she's thinking this is the beginning of something… like I am.

The problem with beginnings is you never know what the ending is going to be. What will happen after she follows me, after she smokes a blunt with me. Maybe she'll figure out there's more to the rich asshole whose family owns the company her father works for. Or maybe she'll think I'm just as shallow as people think I am.

The only way to find out, though, is if she says yes.

Present

Mik is fucking killing me.

Almost literally.

"She has to behave, Son. You get that, right?" My father is perched on the edge of a high-backed chair in my home office, sipping a hundred-dollar glass of cognac.

"Yeah, Dad. I get that." I grip the edge of my desk, letting the sharp corner bite into both my palms. The pain keeps me in the present, prevents me from breaking down.

He's not amused with my plan to clear my name while still getting the girl. Partly, he's annoyed that his plan didn't work. It's normally not hard for my father to cover something up. A few handshakes and nice words usually get the job done. If that doesn't work, cash does.

But even our best publicist couldn't spin the story that is the Wilder family. Once twitter got ahold of their public plea to arrest me, all bets were off.

The public latched onto the story.

Rich family, wild party, dead girl—what's not to love?

The internet was filled with theories. *Rich boyfriend kills sister? Scorned love? Cheating gone wrong?*

None of them figured it out yet though, none of them know the truth of what happened that night.

"People need to embrace you as a loving partner. If she doesn't look completely in love with you, this whole thing will never work." He is so worked up, he downs his drink and uses the back of his hand to wipe at his mouth. I can see the wrinkles in his skin contorting as he frowns. My father has always been good at handling a scandal and keeping his emotions at bay, but this one has him rattled.

Murder charges are a big deal.

"I know," I reply through gritted teeth. I don't need him to tell me how this needs to go, but my father will never pass up an opportunity to lecture me. Grating my nerves is his favorite pastime.

"The way she slammed that door upstairs makes me think that maybe she just doesn't love you," he snarls, his dark eyes penetrating me. My father doesn't like loose ends and Mik knows too much to not comply.

Too much about our business, our family.

I can't stand the man, but on this one, he's right. If

people think that Mik is being forced to be here with me, they'll turn on me even worse. I can see the headlines in my head already. Noah Bancroft: Abuser.

"I'll take care of it," I tell him. My fingers are pressing so hard into the wood that the tips turn white.

If we weren't under a microscope right now, I think my father would just take her family out, a final way to solve our problem. But if the Wilder family went missing now, though? It would cause chaos.

"The tear was a nice touch," my lawyer, David, adds, changing the subject. Probably trying to avoid witnessing an all-out brawl between me and my father.

Dad huffs, pouring himself another glass of cognac.

David readies himself to leave, patting my shoulder on the way out. "Just keep being sensitive and nurturing with her. Let the public know that you love her, and they'll fall in line. And, please, dear Lord, don't let her talk to anyone."

I huff, taking in David's words. He doesn't know Mik like I do. She doesn't want love and nurturing. The girl is wild, a feral animal that can't be tamed.

"You should leave too," I tell my father once David has gone.

I want them all out of here. I want everyone gone. I need another moment alone with Mik, need to feel her underneath me.

I need to fix this.

He huffs, downing the remainder of his cognac and standing up. "I assume I don't need to remind you—"

"Then why are you?" I cut him off.

His dark eyes narrow in on me. "Noah," he sighs. "I will not have my son going to jail, so fix this, or I will, and you won't like how I do it." He slams the rocks glass down on my desk and heads for the door, letting it close loudly behind him.

Finally, I can breathe.

I slump my shoulders, my hands sprawling on the wood of my desk as I suck in a breath of air. My lungs expand for the first time since he walked into my house. I can't stand to be in his presence, but he doesn't give me much of a choice.

He's trying to groom me, his only son, to take over the family business. To learn how to trade in more than money, but in words, backroom deals, and handshakes. The Bancroft Company is my father's life work, an investment firm with a hand in every pot you can think of.

I head upstairs to find Mik, but my room is empty. I told her to stay, not to leave, not to wander, but she listens for shit.

Instead, I find her sprawled out on the guest bed, two rooms away from mine.

She doesn't see me, so I take the moment to revel in her. She looks calmer than she did earlier. Relaxed against the comforter. I lean against the doorframe and watch her.

Damn, how I've missed her. Her sassy mouth, her silly quips. I miss her smile, her laugh. I miss having her in my bed.

I've been missing Mikaela Wilder for almost a whole year now.

"You didn't listen," I say after a moment.

She sits up, propping herself up with her arms and looking at me. "Have I ever?"

I feel a grin rise on my face. "Nope."

She shrugs. "Can I go home?"

"No, baby." I stalk closer to her, sitting on the edge of the bed next to her.

She flips a strand of her blonde hair over her shoulder. It used to be lighter, her roots have grown in and it's clear that she hasn't had it touched up or colored in a while. I wonder if it's been a whole year since she's taken care of herself.

I reach for a piece of it, longing to feel the silky strand between my fingertips, but she flinches and moves away.

"What are you doing, Noah?" Her eyes narrow as she watches my hand retreat back to my lap, unsure of what to expect. She never did.

"I miss you, baby girl," I tell her.

Heat spreads across her cheeks. "I don't miss you," she replies, the lie evident in her trembling fingers.

"You're a liar," I say quietly, not able to rein in my reaction, reaching out to grab her face and turning it back to meet mine. There are tears gathering at the corners of her green eyes, pooling there, waiting to fall. "I know you missed me." I lean in, close enough to get a whiff of her scent, vanilla and honey. She always smells so sweet, and I want to settle into that scent, that comfort. Finding home with her wrapped around me.

She tries to pull her face out of my grip, but I pinch her chin harder, holding her in place.

"You always liked it rough, baby. If I touched you right now, would you be wet for me?"

She hisses, pulling her face out of my grip. "Get the fuck away from me, Noah," she growls, scurrying back, then off the bed, standing so we're on either side of the queen mattress.

I run a hand through my hair. It's long now, unruly. Everything since that night has been harder. I wish I could go back, undo everything. I wish I could make it better.

But I can't.

"What do you need, Mik?" It's a question I'm not sure I've ever asked anyone. "What do you need for me to fix this?"

She stands her ground, arms crossed over her body, drowning in that oversized hoodie of hers. It reminds me of when she used to lounge in my clothes, the loose material a comfort to her and a reminder to me that she's mine.

I wish she would let me comfort her again.

"Space," she says. "Give me space."

A rush of air blows through my lips. "I've given you space, Mik. I've given you tons of space." A whole fucking year of it.

She eyes me. "I'm sorry. I can't just wake up and move on." She throws her hands up in the air dramatically.

"That's not what I'm asking." I scrub a hand over my jaw. "Just let me in."

She laughs, a deep sarcastic sound. "That's rich. Talk to *you* about Auden's death." She shakes her head, placing both hands on her hips. "Just leave, Noah."

For once, I do. I don't argue, I just walk to the door.

"Don't leave." I turn back to tell her. "I have men outside, watching. For your protection," I add.

"So I'm a hostage?" she snarls.

"No, baby, *you're mine.*"

5

mik

There's a moment when I wake up that I forget everything that's happened. It doesn't last long, maybe a few seconds. But in those seconds, I'm happy and my sister is alive.

And then I remember that I'm not happy and Auden is not alive.

Any other morning, I would find a way to numb the pain. But I wake up swaddled in silk sheets under a soft and fluffy comforter and I know I'm not in my dorm room anymore.

There's a bright light shining through the window, telling me it must be morning. It's quiet, and I don't hear Noah moving around, so I'm quick to get up and take care of myself before he wakes up. I want as few reasons to leave this room as possible. I head out into the hallway, to the bathroom. When I'm done, I look both ways before heading down to the kitchen.

My stomach is groaning. I refused dinner last night when Noah came knocking on my door. I didn't want to be near him, didn't want to feel his fingers on my skin. His touch is warm and sends sparks of fire through my body, and I'm not ready to acknowledge what that means yet.

I raid the pantry until I find a tin of muffins, probably something his parents' chef made. Picking apart the blueberry muffin, I feed myself bite-sized pieces.

The front door opens, and I freeze, letting the last bite of pastry sit on my tongue. Noah's eyes find me as soon as he enters the house, with Beckett trailing behind him. The smile that was lingering on his face when he walked in is immediately gone, replaced by a scowl. His eyes scan my body, seeing I'm still in the oversized hoodie from yesterday, except my leggings are gone. I left them up in the room when I wandered out.

"What are you doing?" he asks, his eyes glued to the exposed skin of my legs. His hand rises to his face, his thumb running over his bottom lip. He looks like the big bad wolf, ready to devour me.

I look down at the crumbs from the muffins scattered on a paper towel and then back up to him. "I was—"

"Why aren't you wearing pants?" he asks, his eyebrow ticking, with a hint of a smile in his eyes. Beckett is behind him, a shit-eating grin rising on his face.

The words *I'm sorry* float to the top of my mind, but I stop myself. What a silly thing to say to this man. I'm not doing anything wrong. Hell, I'm the one being held captive. "Fuck you, Noah," I say instead. "I didn't ask to be here."

I want to be back in my dorm room, but I'm not happy there either, just farther away from him.

I'm not happy anywhere, really. I'm a ball of despair rolled into a neat package anywhere I go. For a long time, I didn't smile after Auden died. I lived in misery, pure unhappiness, just going through the motions. It wasn't until months after her death when I was alone in my dorm room, watching some sitcom on cable, that I cracked a smile, a light laugh leaving my lips. It felt good for a quick second until the traitorous feeling settled over me just as fast. Why should I be happy when Auden will never feel joy again?

A lopsided smirk lifts the corner of his lip as he continues to stare at me from the entranceway. "I'll see you later, Beck," he finally says.

Beckett chuckles and spins around. "Bye, Mik," he calls over his shoulder.

"I thought you were sleeping," I mutter, crumpling the dirty napkin in my hand and walking it over to the trash can. I avoid his gaze; I don't want to look at him.

It only takes a few steps for him to stalk over to me, invading my space. "Don't walk around naked." His hand wraps around my arm and he spins me to face him as he growls the words in my ear, a taunting tone lingering between us.

Pushing him off of me is a futile effort, and I barely gain an inch of space. "I'm not *naked*."

Dark eyes wander down to my bare legs again. The hoodie covers most of my ass cheeks, and the tops of my thighs, but the look on his face tells me he doesn't care.

"You're walking around my house without pants on and expecting me to stay away from you." He chuckles softly.

"I don't want you, Noah. Take a hint." I push the palm of my hands against his chest, trying to put space in between us, but it's a futile attempt. He's stronger than me, pressing his hard body against mine, pinning me between him and the counter.

"Mik," he groans. A hand threads through my hair, wrapping around the back of my skull, holding me in place.

"Noah," I respond, trying my best to keep my voice even, an impossible task with his body so close to me.

He sucks in a breath, his dark eyes wandering my face. "You're testing me," he whispers.

I try to shake my head, try to give him a nonverbal answer, but his grip is too tight, making it impossible for me to move. "Noah," I whisper again. "Why am I here?"

His eyes close, and for a moment I think he's sorry. I'm not sure which of his offenses he's feeling guilty about, but his eyes have drifted closed, his mouth soft and tilted in a frown. He looks sad.

"Baby," he drawls. "You belong here."

"I don't." The response leaves my lips quickly. There are few things I'm sure about, but I know this: I'm not meant to be a Bancroft.

I can't show the kind of cruelness that comes with the name.

He tilts his head, his eyes staring into mine. Dark brown meeting green.

"Noah, I have school, and a roommate who is probably wondering where I am. Not to mention my parents..." I trail off.

"I'll take care of it," he says matter-of-factly. There's no arguing with Noah; everything with him is his way. He doesn't see shades of gray or other options. Sometimes I wish I was so sure and confident in myself. In his world, there are no obstacles because money can buy anything... anyone.

I wonder how easy life is when you have money and confidence—does anything bother you?

Surely not murder.

"Noah," I mutter, dropping my gaze. "I can't."

His grip loosens, and he pulls back. "Mik." He looks different when he says my name this time, almost like a part of his defense has dropped. "I need you to trust me, baby." He leans in, our foreheads meeting.

My eyes drift closed, and I lean into him. I can't help it.

How easy it would be to just let everything else drop

away and let him take care of me. If I could just flip off a switch and stop caring.

But then I think of her, bright hazel eyes and auburn hair. I can see her smiling up at me on a sunny day. Her laughter is infectious. My little sister.

She's dead, and I can't let myself be with her killer.

I pull back, farther out of his grip. "Your friends took my phone yesterday. I need it back."

He looks hurt, the sadness still in his eyes. He stares at me for a minute, as if he can't believe I didn't fully lean in and accept him. Like his pretty looks and sweet words should be enough to convince me.

"Sure," he mutters, and stepping back, he rakes a hand through his already messy hair. He looks unshowered, wearing a pair of joggers and a white t-shirt with running shoes.

"What were you and Beckett doing?" I nod to the door.

"Why do you care what I do?" he asks, marching away from me and over to the cabinet in the corner.

"I don't." I nod to the ankle monitor. "But the government does."

He chuckles, pulling my phone out of the drawer and walking back toward me. "Don't worry, Mik, I didn't go too far." He hands me the phone.

I take the device quickly before he changes his mind. "This place is bigger than a prison." I gesture around. "How is that even fair?"

A smirk dances on his lips. "Money, baby. You know that." He leans his body back against the island, his hands flattening against the counter on either side, making the white shirt strain against his muscles.

I remember what that body feels like. I remember all the things it can do.

I feel my mouth drop just a little, and a breathy laugh leaves Noah's lips. "Stop undressing me." He chuckles.

My jaw snaps shut. It only takes me another second to remember where I am. "Noah," I say, trying again. "I can't stay here." I don't want to be in this house. I don't think I can handle the consequences.

My parents will be devastated.

Auden's death was a nuclear bomb to our family. It hit us with no warning, tearing us apart into a million tiny pieces. Even duct tape can't restore the mess her death has created. And I can't blame them for not being able to pull themselves together because I can't either. The youngest daughter, my baby sister, was the glue that held us together, and now all we're left with is a pile of dust that will never be the same.

We're silent as he assesses me. "Your parents?" he asks, reading my mind. I nod, and a harsh breath escapes his lips. "They should have never posted that video."

"What were they supposed to do?" I retort. Truthfully, I begged them not to post it. Mostly, I didn't want to believe it. I still struggle to. One day, I was madly in love, about to marry this man. And the next, my parents were accusing him of murder. It was a hard pill to swallow.

"Not that." He eyes me sternly. "Do you remember anything from that night?" he asks, slightly changing the subject from my parents.

I shake my head. My memories from that night are foggy. Pools of dark water that I can't break through. At first, I tried. I wanted nothing more than to remember what happened to my sister, but after a while, I figured it was better if I didn't.

"Probably good." Noah moves his gaze from me.

"Will you tell me?" I ask. It's a question I've asked before.

He shakes his head, pushing himself off the counter and walking back over to me. "I've told you."

"It feels... like I'm missing something."

He invades my space, wrapping his arms around me. "I told you, baby. Don't rack your brain trying to bring back memories that are only going to hurt you." He presses his lips against my forehead, and I lean into his comfort.

I want to hate him, I really do.

But I let him hold me and kiss me softly, and I remember all the reasons I love him.

"Mik." He pulls back just a little, his hot breath hitting my skin as he whispers my name. "Just let me take care of you, baby girl. Please, just trust me."

His voice is soft, and I'm flooded with memories of us together. We were good together, I think. We were happy at one time.

I long for that feeling of happiness again, and with him right here, I can almost taste it on my tongue.

"Yeah," I whisper back. "I can do that."

6

mik

Halloween Night, One Year Earlier

"What kind of party is it?" Auden asks from the passenger seat of my Volkswagen Beetle, the small car barely fitting her poofy dress.

I shrug. "Something with his family, I guess. A big Halloween party." Noah and his group of friends throw lots of parties, mostly at their own houses because what's being a rich twenty-four-year-old if you aren't throwing bangers in your expensive house?

Tonight, though, Noah told me to be ready for a party at his parents' home. The Bancroft house is a large estate hidden far off the main streets. It feels like a luxurious country club spread across far too much land. With Noah not living there, the house seems too large for just two people.

"Why wasn't Dad invited?" she asks. Our father is high enough in the hierarchy at Bancroft Co. that he normally gets invited to all the gatherings.

"I don't know," I tell her. "Maybe this one's just for the inner circle?"

The "inner circle" is the name we gave to the four families. Made up of four super wealthy families, they have more of a hand in Washington than most people probably realize.

The Bancrofts, Radcliffes, Monroes, and Wolfes.

Also known as the families of Noah and his four closest friends.

It sounds like the beginning to a lame joke: what happens when you get an investment banker, a real estate developer, the CEO of a media conglomerate, and a senator in a room together? They become best friends and take over D.C.

"You look pretty," she says, and I know she means it because Auden doesn't do sarcasm.

I'm not good at meeting the standards of Noah's family. They want a picture-perfect trophy wife for him, not the state college educated daughter of one of their employees. Still, Noah dates me.

Tonight, I'm wearing a simple black dress that drops low in the front, showing off my cleavage, and a pair of over the knee black heeled boots. My lips are coated in black lipstick and there's a majestic set of black angel wings in the trunk. I don't know how rich people do Halloween, but I'm thinking this is it.

"Thanks." I toss her a smile. It's not that I dislike Auden; when it's just us, we're fine. She's just the perfect youngest child, and being her older sister can be challenging sometimes. "What are you and Kelly doing tonight?"

She flashes me a sly smile. "If I tell you… can you not tell Mom and Dad?"

I slap my hand over my heart in shock. "Are you, Auden Elizabeth Wilder, the perfect child, about to do something bad?" I ask with a smile.

She laughs. "Just a party with some kids from school."

"Will there be alcohol there?"

"Probably." She shrugs. "But you know me. I won't drink that."

"Sure." I laugh. Auden is a goody two-shoes, so I'm surprised she would even consider going to a party at all. "Just be safe, hmm?" I use my elbow to nudge her.

"I will," she says. "Mik," she adds after a moment. "What is sex like?" A blush rises to her cheeks as she asks me the question. My sister is a sweet, sweet virgin. She's the definition of innocent.

"Auden." I inhale sharply. "Are you—"

"I don't know," she cuts me off, looking intimidated and nervous as she stares at the road ahead.

"Auden," I say, lower, more serious. "Don't do anything you're not ready for. You should take your time."

She sighs, twisting her fingers in her lap. "I know, but I think I want to... I'm just scared, ya know?"

I know. I think about my own first time in the back of a pickup truck when we lived in North Carolina. It was with a kid from school who was fumbling and nervous. It was bad all around. But isn't everyone's first time bad? Aren't we all just a mess trying to figure this shit out?

"Listen," I tell her. "First times are weird. It's a mess of figuring out how everything works and what feels good. But once you get past that, sex can be incredible." I take a deep breath. It's weird describing this to my little sister. It feels dirty and wrong, even though I've since gotten past the idea that sex is anything other than pleasurable. "It's like..." I trail off, trying to come up with the best way to describe the feeling.

I look around, seeing that the main strip of road we're on is mostly empty. We're sitting at the red light, waiting on the change of color to move forward. A push of a button brings my sunroof down, letting the cool night air filter through the car. Another push brings down our windows.

"Hold on," I tell her with a smile. When the light turns green, I hit the gas pedal, and my Beetle lurches forward with the speed. I keep my foot on the gas until we're flying.

Auden grabs on the handlebar at the passenger door like she's holding on for dear life. "Mikaela!" she shouts.

"This is it!" I yell back. "It's fast, and crazy, and fucking freeing." The next light in front of us turns red, and I press the brake, slowing us down until we stop in front of the light with a quick jerk.

Auden's screams turn to laughter, and soon we're both howling until we're in tears.

She looks at me with a wide smile and watery eyes. "You're insane." She laughs.

Present

I push the memories of Auden from my mind.

She's haunting me.

It's worse than normal, as if being in Noah's house is forcing things back to the top of my mind. I can't shake the thoughts of her, of everything that's happened.

There are fifty missed calls when I turn my phone back on. Mostly from my parents.

"Are you okay?" The call only rings once before my mom picks up, the question leaving her lips in a rush.

"I'm fine," I tell her, trying my best to keep my voice even.

"Mikaela, I've been so worried!" Her voice is shrill and panicked, and I can hear my father in the background, asking if it's me on the phone.

Guilt bubbles up in my chest, a pain running through me. "I'm sorry," I mutter.

"It's okay, just tell me where you are? Are you all right?" Her voice is strained, worried. My heart aches knowing how much pain I've put them through.

"I'm with Noah," I whisper.

As I speak his name, I see him linger in the doorway to the guest room. He's keeping his distance, letting me talk to my mom, but he's there watching me.

"I know," she says softly. "I saw the show."

The way she says the word "show" feels like a bullet to my chest. She's not wrong though, that's what it was. All a show, a ploy to make the public fall for Noah, the sweet, doting fiancé.

Even so, I look up at him standing in the doorway in his black joggers, white t-shirt tight against his chest. His dark eyes are watching me, and even though it should feel ominous, I feel safe.

I probably shouldn't, but I can't help it.

"I'm sorry," I whisper, repeating myself.

"Mikaela, tell me what's going on? Why are you with him?" she pleads.

I don't know what to tell her. I shouldn't be here. I should walk out, tell him to fuck off. He's barely given me a reason to stay, been nothing but demanding since he dragged me here. Still, he asked me to trust him, and I said yes.

My gaze flashes to the ring on my nightstand. The huge fucking rock. How many times have I looked at my bare finger over the past year and felt empty?

Hollow.

"I'm okay," I try to reassure her. "I'm just... I'm good here, okay? Let me just... I need to figure this out." I whisper the last part. I need to figure a lot out. What happened that night, to me, to Auden. I know I'm breaking my mother's heart, pushing the boundaries of her morals.

I hear her sniffle, and I'm afraid she's trying to hide her tears from me on the other end. "Okay," she whispers. "I trust you, Mikaela, but please call me if you need me. And text me to let me know you're okay."

"I will," I tell her, trying my best to hold my own tears in.

We hang up and I set my phone off to the side. My parents have been broken since Auden's death, but also overprotective of me. Almost as if they fear the same thing will happen to me. Since they believe Noah's the reason behind Auden's death, I can't blame them for not wanting me here.

I can't explain why I think they're wrong, why some part of me still trusts Noah even though everyone around me thinks I'm wrong.

"You okay?" he asks, still standing in the doorway, watching over me.

I nod. "Yeah, I think so."

He stalks into the room slowly, coming to the edge of the bed where I'm sitting and hovering over me. His palm reaches for my cheek, warming the cool skin on my face. I find myself leaning into his touch.

"I'm sorry this is so hard for you, baby girl," he whispers. "If I could take away your pain, I would."

I believe him when he says it, but what he fails to realize is, he is my pain. He forced his way into my life and set me ablaze, lighting up my world until everything about me was burning in his hot flames. Then, just as quickly, it all turned to ash.

"We'll get through this, baby. You just have to trust me." He leans in and kisses my forehead softly, the gesture giving me goosebumps. "Do you trust me?" he asks.

I don't respond, instead I stay silent while he kisses my forehead, the tip of my nose, and down to my lips. He's leaning down now so his face is directly in front of mine. Do I trust him? A year ago, I would have said I trusted him with my life. Love isn't strong enough of a word to describe how I felt about Noah Bancroft. Now? I'm not so sure.

"Mikaela," he says, using my full name, something he only does when he's being serious. I'm normally baby, baby girl, or Mik. "Answer me, baby. Do you trust me?"

I nod.

The gesture feels final, absolute. Like I'm sealing my fate with just a gesture of my head.

"Words, baby girl." His deep voice sends a shiver down my spine. He wants me to say the words, confirm my destiny, removing any inkling of doubt.

"Yes." I don't know if it's true. I'm doubting myself. Doubting him. I'm not sure who I believe anymore. My parents are certain he's to blame, and for a while, I was too. I'm not sure it's not him, but even so, I can't help the way my body responds to him.

My nipples harden, pebbling underneath the fabric of my top. My core tightens and I know he can tell I'm turned on just by the sound of his voice when he talks to me.

I like him like this.

Demanding.

Controlling.

I want to pretend I don't. I want to think I'm a strong woman. But I melt when he puts his hands on me and whispers in my ear. When he tells me what to do.

I'm putty in his palms.

He's not my hero, I know that. He'll never be my knight in shining armor. He won't swoop me into his arms and save me from danger. He's my villain, with dark hair and a sinful smile.

"What are you thinking about, baby girl?" he asks, the tip of his finger drawing a line from my temple down my cheek, sending a spark with it. He traces down my jawline to my throat, my collarbone. He lingers at the hem of my hoodie. "Tell me."

"You," I whisper. That's the truth. He fills my mind, his presence always lingering in my head. I can't shake the thought of him, and when I finally do, I feel dead inside.

I'm a sucker for him. For his words, his pretty face—everything about him has me hooked. His hand drifts to my face, palming my cheek. His warmth permeates me.

He grins. "Yeah, baby?"

I nod, which only encourages him to continue, but I'm already in too deep. I feel my layers melting away, stripping me bare for him. I've always belonged to Noah Bancroft.

"Take this off." He pulls on the strings of the hoodie.

"Noah—" I start to talk, to stop this, to use words to bring me out of the haze I'm surrounded by.

"Don't think, baby, just let me take care of you." His words float from his lips, and I want to believe him. I want to be here in this moment instead of stuck in my head, over-analyzing every detail.

I frown, unsure. Two days ago, I was certain that Noah was a bad guy. It was only this morning that he started to twist up my feelings, making me unsure of myself. If I let him in now, I'm afraid he'll wreck me.

"You're overthinking," he whispers, and he's not wrong.

I pull the hoodie over my head, exposing myself to him. I have nothing but a pair of panties underneath. I'm naked in front of him, but it feels like more than that. I feel bare, exposed. This gesture, this one move, is changing everything, warping it. I don't know what tomorrow will bring after this.

He hums his approval, his hand trailing down to my tits,

cupping one of them in his palm. He rolls my nipple between his fingers, sending a spark through my body. "Lay back, baby."

I listen. Pushing all of my fears and doubts aside, I lay back and just let myself feel. Hands rub up my thighs softly, caressing me. The motion is comforting, and I find myself relaxing into his touch. Heat courses through my body and I know I'm already wet for him, turned on just by his light touches, his simple words.

He likes to trick me like that, give me soft, comforting motions, ease me in before he snakes his hand up and around my throat. I think I should be scared, but it's never scared me. It's only had the opposite effect.

Even now, as one hand lightly presses on my windpipe and the other drifts down under my panties, I'm not scared, and I don't hate him.

Instead, I allow him to explore my body, a body he knows well. We were never innocent when we were together. It was always rough and passionate. Hard kisses against brick walls. His hand between my legs and his belt around my neck. We were never soft, and I never wanted to be.

"You're so fucking beautiful," he mumbles, then his mouth presses against mine, teeth biting down on my bottom lip.

The mixture of pain with pleasure heightens every sensation. As the air becomes more difficult to breathe in, a slight pinch from his fingers digging into my throat, I grow needier for him. I want him more, the more it hurts.

"You're wet for me, baby girl." He pulls back enough to flash me a sexy grin as his fingers slip through my folds. He drags my wetness up to my clit, swirling it around my swollen nub.

A moan escapes my lips, and I can't help myself. I've

been without him for almost a year and even hate doesn't erase need. And I need him. My body longs for his touch, fire licking across my skin as his fingertips dance along my curves.

A smile plays on his lips as he slips a finger into me while his thumb circles over my clit. "You missed me?" he asks.

"Yeah." The word leaves my lips in a husky whisper. I'm hot beneath him, my heart racing. Everything else, all the drama and pain, have slipped from my mind, leaving nothing but this moment.

He picks up the pace, adding a second finger until I'm writhing beneath him. The hand around my throat squeezes tighter, cutting off my air supply. I only grow hotter.

"Show me, baby. Show me how much you missed me." His dark voice drifts over me.

I'm shaking now as he continues, his dirty words filling my ears as one hand wraps around my throat and the other circles my clit. I'm drowning in the sensation, overtaken by the closeness of my release.

"Mik," he whispers in my ear, and I'm so close I know I'm about to do anything he says to get the release I'm dying for. "Come for me, baby."

I'm surrounded by a foggy haze; there's nothing but him and I. I crash over the edge of my orgasm with a loud cry and his name on my lips.

"Fuck," I mutter as the sensations start to wind down. The room starts to come back to me, the reality of our situation settling back in. Sweat trickles down my skin and a dull ache grows in my head.

Noah pulls his fingers from me, bringing them to his lips and sucking the taste of me off of them. "Now, baby," he says, a slight growl to his voice, "put that fucking ring back on your finger."

7

noah

Three Years Earlier

"Where are we going?" Mikaela asks me as I lead her back to the outside. My parents are throwing another one of their ungodly corporate parties. The ones where they show off all their money, lording their status over everyone in their circles.

The guests are dressed in suits and ties, standing under the hot sun on the oversized patio. Heels clack against the custom pavers my mother had installed. Her favorite part of throwing parties is showing off all the nice things she has.

I lead Mikaela past the pergola, past the patios, past the garden that my mother pays people to tend to. The Bancroft property is huge, more land than we could ever need. The estate is propped up on a hill, back further than all the other houses in the area.

"Wow," Mikaela whispers, her voice rushing out in amazement. I study her. Her pupils are wide as she takes in the sight. Her arms have dropped, no longer in her annoyed stance. She's focused on the scene in front of us, her expression one of pure bewilderment.

I've seen it a million times, but still, even I can't get over the beauty. At the back of my parents' land is a high cliff overlooking deep blue water. Straight below, about a thirty-foot drop, is a small beach, completely inaccessible. From here, all you see are the tan and orange pebbles and a small pocket of sand.

"This is my favorite spot," I tell her, stuffing my hands in my pockets.

Her head turns to look at me, her green eyes meeting mine.

"It's beautiful," she whispers.

There are no chairs out this far. The party feels like it's miles away, even if we can still hear the music and voices lingering in the distance. Lights strung up around the property are glowing brightly as golden hour sets. The view is even more stunning at this time of day.

I lower myself to the ground, not far from the cliff's edge, and pull the blunt I rolled earlier free from my pocket. Mikaela sits next to me, her eyes still glued to the view.

"I come here a lot, to think and stuff."

"Is that why you brought me here?" she asks, a small smile at the edges of her lips. "To think?"

"Nah." I lean forward, resting my head on my hand as I look at her. She's pretty, one of those girls who looks effortless but probably puts effort into her appearance. "I don't think I'll be able to think with you around."

There's a slight pink that rises to her cheeks and she bits her bottom lip like she's trying to keep it from smiling. I like it.

"Smooth," she says. "Bet you say that to all the girls."

I bark out a laugh. "Nope." I grin. "You're the first."

In this moment, everything shifts. I feel something here,

between us. I can only imagine the picture, the two of us staring into each other's eyes with the waves crashing in the distance.

I want to know Mikaela Wilder.

Present

"Is she ready?" Vaughn's voice drifts through the EarPods I'm wearing. I moved my laptop out to the kitchen island so I could watch for Mik while I work.

"Noah?" Vaughn calls, his voice ringing in my ears.

"Yeah, man, I heard you. I think so." I shove a hand through my hair, pulling on the dark locks. It's too long. My mother wanted to send someone over to cut it yesterday, but I told her not to. I wanted to look a little more rugged, like I haven't been awaiting trial in a fucking mansion. I needed to be relatable, and the neatly groomed Noah is not relatable at all.

Vaughn scoffs. "You think so?"

"Yeah, I know." I don't need him to tell me how stupid this plan is. It's genius, but only if it works and the chance that it doesn't work is… troubling.

Mik is a wild card, so trusting my life to her is not my brightest idea. She's always had… issues, mood swings, paranoid moments. I don't think there's a therapist in the world that would give her mental health an A-plus rating. She struggles, more often than not, but most of the time, I can handle it. I can deal with her ups and downs, and most of the time, she can too. She hasn't processed Auden's death though, something she needs to get through or else this plan might not have a chance.

"It will work," I tell him. I'm hoping it will, and I'm hanging onto the sliver of hope that Mik believes in me.

"Okay," Vaughn huffs. "Let me know what you need from me."

I thank him and hang up quickly. I hate rehashing this with him, with my father, or David. Repeating the same things over and over again. Constantly telling them that I trust her.

They just need to trust me.

It's been hours by the time Mik emerges from the guest room. Her hair is wet and hanging down in damp waves. A pair of dark jeans cover her legs, and a loose t-shirt hangs from her torso. She's never been one to wear tight clothing, to actively work to be attractive every minute of the day. Unlike every other woman I've known, every girl my parents tried to set me up with. Mikaela never lies to others or herself. She owns her feelings and doesn't change her appearance for anyone.

Different from the girl who slowly peeks out of her room, looking both ways. She's guarded now, scared, broken. I watch her from the shadows as she takes every step lightly, barely making a sound, as if even the tiniest noise could wreck everything.

She's not the strong, stubborn woman I once knew.

I wanted to give her time. Time to heal, to move on, time to just be away from me.

I wanted to let her breathe.

But it seems time didn't do her any good.

What has she been doing? Living with ghosts stuck in her head, probably. Revisiting the same night over and over again. She says she doesn't remember anything, and I wonder if that's true. She was so fucking out of it when I found her, so far gone. I can't get the picture of her out of my mind.

I shake it off, willing myself to stop revisiting those memories. Instead, I tuck them away, far back in my head, storing them and hoping to never see them again.

I wanted her to be fine without me, I really did. We crashed and burned, both of us walking away in pieces.

But she's not better without me, and I'm no good without her.

So we're stuck together, and we're fucking dead apart.

She could devastate me. She could set my entire world on fire.

Or she could be the one to save me.

I watch her peek her head into the kitchen, as expected, her eyes wandering over my body before they find my face.

"Hi." I smirk.

She seems shy under my gaze, or nervous maybe. She doesn't speak, slowly wandering into the kitchen.

"You can't wear that," I tell her.

Her eyes meet mine. "Why?" she questions.

I shake my head. Earlier, I told her to get ready and dress nice, so her jeans and t-shirt feel like she's actively disobeying me.

"Where are we going?" she presses.

"Mikaela," I sigh. I can't tell her, not yet. "You said you would trust me, hmm?"

She huffs, a breath of air rushing from her lips. "It goes both ways," she mutters, spinning on her heel.

"Something nice," I call, and I know it makes me sound like an asshole. "A dress, heels, ya know."

I hear her mutter something under her breath as she marches up the stairs. I'm sure it's a slur about me. But that's fine. She can hate me as long as she does it in private.

Once we leave this house, our act has to be perfect. Flawless. Everyone around us needs to believe that she's in love with me and there's no way I killed her sister, or else this entire charade goes to hell.

I watch her walk away from me, her hips swaying as she goes up the stairs.

I'm going to break her today.

I don't know what that makes me. The monster, the villain. I'm surely not the hero in her story.

I scrub a hand over my face. My heart is pounding in my chest, a rapid beat thrumming along with the anxiety of what I'm about to do to her.

It's the right thing, I know that. Still, the thought of seeing her face when she figures this all out is breaking me apart.

Steadying myself, I inhale a deep breath and let the oxygen fill me up.

I'm going to break her.

8

mik

Halloween Night - One Year Earlier

I pull my Beetle through the gates of the Bancroft estate. Even after two years of visiting this house, I still scoff as I pass through the wrought iron passageway bearing the family name.

Only rich people have gates with their names on them.

It's not even that my family is poor; we're upper middle class, but we don't have wealth like this. Though, to be fair, most people in America don't have wealth like this. Only one percent of Americans hold fifty percent of the country's wealth, and the Bancrofts are in that one percent. Who knew investment banking paid so damn well?

I'm reminded of this fact every day with Noah. People look at him when we're together, recognizing him off lists of wealthy businessmen, knowing him as the son of "that guy." And then the looks turn to me; the poor girl with ripped jeans and no trust fund. It makes for awkward dinners and uncomfortable family conversations.

When it's just us though, just Noah and Mikaela—things are different.

His friends aren't bad either, the lot of them. Other sons of wealthy people, who will never want for anything. Still, even with money, they're just young assholes who think they own the world.

Except, maybe they do.

I leave my car parked out front and hand the keys off to the valet. Even for what Mariam calls a "small get-together," there's a valet, a caterer, and a musician. Mariam doesn't throw dull parties, that's for sure.

Grabbing the rest of my costume from the trunk, I secure the large black wings to the back of my dress, taking a second to admire them through the dark windows of my car.

Dad helped to make the large wire frame and then covered it with black feathers, dipping each one in glitter. The wings are large, sparkly, and beautiful. Paired with my black dress, knee-high boots, and lipstick—I look dark and deadly.

"Mikaela!" Vaughn calls as I enter through the grand foyer, clicking my heels against the marble floor. A beer is wrapped in his fist, dripping condensation from his fingers while he opens both arms wide, pulling me in for a hug.

Of the four boys, Vaughn is probably the most responsible. He's in his last year of law school and already has a job lined up in D.C. for when he's done. But law school must take its toll because he's also the first of us to get wasted. Though the stress doesn't help, I'm sure. The constant pressure of his family's expectations looming over his head.

When you're rich, connections start to mean almost as much as money and the best ones are family connections. What better way to join a family than marry into it?

Everyone in their social circle does it, all of that one

percent. They pawn off their kids, trade them away for status and power.

It's like a game.

I shoot Vaughn a pitiful look, the same one I always give. The dissatisfaction hangs on him; he's a shell of himself under that burden of responsibility. I can't imagine what that feels like, what it's like to live this life. People think money buys happiness, but when I look at Noah and these boys, I think that's a lie. Money can buy things you enjoy, sure, but that only covers up the pain like a blanket. Just hiding it from view, but it's still there, deep in the darkness.

He pulls back, pressing a kiss to each of my cheeks dramatically. "Noah! Mikaela's here," he calls, his words slurring, and I can tell he's already had too many drinks. Someone will be around to chastise him soon, scolding him for getting too loose. You can't let your guard down, ever.

The house is filled, probably fifty to seventy people here. I see Mariam flutter by in an elegant gown with a chic mask. Mariam isn't one to miss an opportunity to look amazing, drenched in a rich red color with an extravagant mask made of feathers, glitter and gems.

The house is decorated extravagantly with dark fabrics and crystal balls. Skulls dipped in gold litter the surfaces, along with vases of black roses. I soak in the dark vibes, the witchy elegance. I love the theme of it all.

"Hey, beautiful." Strong arms wrap around my waist, pulling me against a hard body. I feel Noah move his lips from my ears down to the crook of my neck, his grip still tight around me. He smells like black coffee and cedarwood, and I inhale the scent, letting it wash over me.

I tilt my head, smiling up at him. His black hair is curling slightly at the edges, and it falls in his face when he looks down at me. His lips press against the tip of my nose as we hold that position. "I missed you," he whispers.

"You saw me yesterday." I laugh, spinning out of his grip and turning to face him.

"So long ago." He pouts, pushing out his bottom lip at me.

I feel special in his arms. His words, his voice, everything about him pulls me in, wrapping me in warmth and happiness. It's not lost on me that I don't fit into his world easily. We're puzzle pieces that have been warped. We should fit; the picture is absolutely perfect, but we don't slide into place next to each other. It takes work to fit the two pieces together.

The thought has passed through my mind that I'm just a phase for him, the poor girl he'll date for a moment and then toss to the curb once the thrill has worn off. At first, I expected the other shoe to drop. I guarded myself, waiting for that inevitable break-up, but it never came.

Slowly, he broke down all my walls, chipping away at them until I was laid bare before him. I feel safe in his arms, happy with him. I lean into his warm embrace, seeking comfort in him.

"What are you?" Noah asks, pulling back from me and letting his eyes wander over my outfit.

"An angel." I grin. "But a dark one."

NOAH DRIVES US TODAY. I spare a glance at his ankle monitor as we head to the car. The thick, black plastic cuff around his ankle is clearly visible underneath the bottom of his black dress pants.

"It's fine, Mik." He chuckles, reading my mind. "I'm allowed to leave the house, as long as I get it approved," he tells me as he walks around to the passenger side of his matte black Mercedes S-Class. A grin is etched on his face as he swings the door open for me, ever the gentleman.

I hum softly under my breath, mulling over this new piece of information. So this is an approved venture. I wonder if anyone else gets to leave their house while fighting murder charges, or if this is something that just applies to the rich. Hell, most people wouldn't even get bail or an ankle monitor. They would probably be tossed in a cell with the key thrown away. I can't even keep track of how many horror stories I've heard where people get thrown behind bars with no due process.

Not Noah, though.

Never Noah.

His family has too much money.

"You look good," he tells me, his eyes scanning my body as I sit down in the passenger seat, feeling the soft leather beneath my bare thighs. I picked a navy-blue dress from the closet full of clothes, which I'm assuming are all supplied by Mariam or her personal shopper. The dress hits slightly above my knees with buttons down the front and ties at my waist. It's modest and pretty and felt appropriate for what he wanted.

His dark eyes linger on me for an extra moment, and approval coats his features. His family is all about appearances. Aesthetics. They like to look good, always on trend, never a hair out of place.

The Bancrofts put on a show, an act. Everything that can be seen of them is fake, a conceived lie to make them look perfect.

I'm one of those things now, I know. An object in their game, dolled up to fit their needs.

I barely know who I am anymore, my chest a hollow cave, my brain empty. Grief comes in waves. I'm told there are five stages, but mine are all over the place.

Denial.
Depression.
Anger.
Depression.
Bargaining.
More Anger.
Lots of depression.

Depression is my one constant, the thing that stays with me the most. My best friend and closest confidante. I curl up in bed with it, letting it sink its claws deep into everything I am, everything I know, until I'm nothing but a deep, dark void of emptiness. My bones melt away, my body feels far off, my mind shuts down, and I sink away into nothingness. Sometimes that's better, when everything shuts off. I enjoy having the reprieve from the anxiety, not having to think about all the reasons I'm here. Sometimes the depression is just better.

The last stage is acceptance, but I haven't felt that one yet. I've convinced myself it's a lie, a cruel joke created to make me think that one day I'll feel better. One day, this will all pass.

But I don't think it ever will. I don't think there will ever be a day I wake up and don't feel fucking empty inside.

Noah slides into the seat next to me, pressing the start button and bringing the engine to life. His Mercedes is nothing like my old Beetle. The engine purrs a soft sound, the seats are smooth beneath me, and a large screen sits in the center, between us. This car screams money.

I twist my fingers in my lap as he navigates us out of the gated community and out onto the road. My anxiety is threatening to claw its way out of my chest. I'm spiraling with all the thoughts of where we could be going, not knowing which one it might be.

"Breathe." Noah's voice sounds beside me, making me

flinch and pulling me from the depths of my mind. "I can practically hear you spiraling," he adds. "It's *fine*, Mik."

I want to believe him. I want to trust him. I want more than anything to push away all my fears and thoughts and just sink into Noah.

But I've done that before, and it didn't work out.

"You loved me once," he says, his voice a hushed whisper. I'm not sure if he's talking to me, or thinking aloud from how soft his voice is.

"I did," I tell him, my eyes focused on the road, trying to ignore the bob of his throat and the solemn look on his face.

I loved him in ways that I never expected. I wasn't looking for anything when he walked into my life, and suddenly, I was wrapped up in all things Noah. He made me laugh, held me close. Being with him was pure light and happiness. Flickers of our relationship float through my mind like a montage from a rom-com.

He was my everything, my euphoria.

And then he was nothing.

"It doesn't just stop," he murmurs. His sad voice penetrates my soul. My love for him still runs deep, even with everything going on. My hate is just a Band-Aid. Stopping my feelings for him would be like someone gutting me; it's not an easy thing. I can't just turn it on and off, but I can't let him know that.

"Where are we going, Noah?" My voice comes out sadder, whinier than I intend, and Noah sighs heavily.

For a moment, it looks like he's carrying the weight of the world on his shoulders. He looks overtaken with grief and sorrow, then, just as quickly, he pushes it all aside, slipping his perfectly tailored mask back into place.

"You trust me, Mik?" he asks. It's a loaded question, one he asked me before and I told him, yes. He pulls in a deep breath and slowly releases it. I can feel the conflict radiating off him. He's torn.

When I don't answer, he continues. "I need you to trust me, baby. What I'm going to ask you to do in there is going to be hard, but it's important. Can you trust me?"

As he asks the question, he navigates the Mercedes into a parking lot in front of a tall building covered in glass windows from bottom to top. The sign reads McKinley & Sons. It's a law firm.

"What are we doing?" I ask, the words leaving my lips rushed and frantic.

The anxiety is welling back up inside me.

"Mik." He places his hand on mine, the warmth permeating me, bringing me comfort.

There are flashes outside the car, the press settled in front of the building.

Another fucking publicity stunt.

"You don't have to say anything, baby." He turns my face to meet his with the tips of his fingers. His other hand still rests on mine.

Another flash.

They're taking photos of us through the windshield of the Mercedes.

"You just have to walk in with me. Stay close to me." He looks down at me, his hand rising to rest on my cheek.

"It's a show," I mouth. I can feel the tears welling in my eyes.

"Trust me," he says again. Those words seem to leave his lips a lot lately. He looks serious as he reaches forward, swiping away a stray tear.

Flash.

The cameras catch his comforting motions. "You can do this, Mik." We're not far from the entrance, only a few steps, I think. I steel my spine and ready myself. Noah jumps from the car, running around from my side to open the door and help me out.

Flash.

He wraps an arm around me, trying to shield me from the cameras, and we rush to the entrance. I can feel their eyes on me, and I wonder what they're thinking.

A victim with a murderer?

If I wasn't me, if I was on the outside watching this, I think I would judge me too. I would shout out to this girl, asking her why she's with the man who killed her sister? Why is she letting him touch her, protect her?

Why does she trust him?

On the surface, it may be that simple, but it's really more complex than that. Intricate layers, history that interconnects us.

I wish I could write off Noah Bancroft, but the truth is, I really do trust him.

David, the same lawyer from the press conference, is waiting for us when we enter. His eyes drift to me first, looking over my appearance, checking to make sure I fit the image.

David looks perfectly made in a tailored navy-blue suit with a white shirt and a silky silver tie. He reminds me of the lawyer you see in movies, hair slicked back, suit wrinkle-free. His voice floats from his lips in a deep tenor and he speaks like he knows everything.

He looks pleased as he moves his gaze to Noah, extending his hand for a quick shake. "Good," he says. "They're upstairs."

"Who?" I blurt out the question, more to Noah than David, but both sets of eyes look to me.

"Trust me, remember?" Noah says, his eyebrow raising in a questioning manner.

I inhale deeply and try to calm my fried nerves. I trust

him. I repeat the words in my head over and over again, begging myself to believe them, but it's hard to trust him when I don't know what the plan is.

We're playing a game, and it feels like everyone else knows the rules but me.

David leads us to the elevator, hitting the button for the 17th floor and taking us up. "It's a deposition." Noah tells me once the elevator is steadily rising.

A deposition. The word spins in my head, not quite sure what he means.

David must spot my confusion. "Part of the pre-trial discovery," he murmurs.

It clicks.

I knew he was flaunting me around as a publicity stunt, but this is gold. Having me on his arm as he enters his pre-trial hearings is a show of my support.

My belief in his innocence.

I feel used and dumb. Hurt radiates through my body, but I knew what I was getting myself into. I should have seen this, should have known.

"Hey," Noah whispers, palming my cheek with his warm hand. "It's gonna be okay."

I don't know if I believe that. He asked me to trust him, and I'm trying, but I think believing everything is going to be okay is pushing it.

I'm not sure we'll ever be okay again.

9

noah

Three Years Earlier

I avoid doing anything fancy when I take Mik out for the first time. It's a Friday night and we're near her college, the one she just started her freshman year at.

I think she's surprised when I pull up to the Shake Shack, but I see a smile tug at the corners of her mouth.

"Burgers?" she muses, the question dripping from her tongue with interest. I know what she thinks of me, mostly because she wasn't shy about sharing her opinion.

I'm privileged, rich, an asshole.

And all of those things are true, but there's more underneath the mask.

"They're good," I tell her, grinning.

A laugh escapes from her mouth, her chest shaking with the noise. "You're weird," she tells me, but it doesn't sound like an insult.

A fucking compliment, actually. An acknowledgement that she sees through me, sees a part of me very few ever have.

We order way too much food when we reach the front of the line. Burgers, cheese fries, and milkshakes. I lead her to a booth in the back, one farther away from people. I want her all to myself, every moment of her. Every single smile, laugh, word, they're mine for the taking.

I try to reel in the dominance, not let the hold she has on me show, but it's there.

She's fucking mine.

She slips into the booth, the metal on the back of her ripped black jeans scratching across the vinyl seat. She has on a black t-shirt with the name of some band scribbled on it and her pale hair is piled on top of her head messily.

"You're staring at me," she says, an amused edge to her voice.

She drums her chipped fingernails against the table as we stare at each other, still sizing the other one up, not quite sure what this is or where it's going.

"So... school..." I trail off, not sure what to ask her. I'm normally much more confident, put together, but this girl throws me off my axis.

She snorts a laugh at my attempted conversation before swiping a delicate finger through the loose hairs falling in her face. "Yep," she says with a pop. "I go to school, good talk." Her words come out laced with sarcasm, but there is a sweet smile dancing on her lips. She's amused with me, toying with me. She feels the sparks between us, and even though she's trying to maintain her aloof attitude, I know she's excited too.

I snort a laugh back at her and pop a fry into my mouth. Energy courses through my body with just a tinge of anxiety. I feel like she's woken me up from a haze.

"So, pretty boy," she drawls. "What do rich kids do for fun anyway?" She crosses her ankles under her legs in the booth and leans her elbows onto the vinyl tabletop. My mother would faint if she saw her sitting like that, so fucking unladylike in public.

But blood rushes to my dick at the sight.

I quirk a brow, eyeing her suspiciously. "Why? Are you trying to get in trouble?" I ask, shoving another fry slathered in cheese sauce into my mouth.

Mik isn't shy about eating either. She unwraps the burger, bringing the dripping sandwich to her lips and taking a large bite. I watch as she chews, a little bit of sauce dripping from her lip.

The whole thing looks sensual, and I have to fucking calm myself down. She's eating a damn burger, for Christ's sake. It isn't erotic, but with her, everything feels that way.

Like she's putting on a show specially catered to me.

And I'm loving every fucking minute of it.

"Maybe," she answers between bites.

I chuckle, unwrapping my own burger. "What kind of trouble are you looking to get into, baby girl?"

She grins up at me, her green eyes meeting mine through thick black lashes. "The worst kind," she tells me.

Fuck, I think I might just love this girl.

MIK'S FACE IS ASHEN, pale and terrified.

I knew the idea of looking like a loving partner would be hard for her, but the look on her face is tragic. Her eyes are glassy, their normal green shade now something darker, filled with pain.

Guilt is clawing its way through me, and I want to stop what I'm doing and hold her, comfort her. But I also need to protect her, and this will do just that. I have to remind myself what the goal here is. I can't do anything for her if I'm behind bars.

I slip my mask back on and steel my spine, readying myself for whatever comes next. David spent weeks preparing me for this deposition. My story is solid, my lies are impenetrable.

He gives me a look, a silent question asking if I'm ready.

I am.

I press a chaste kiss to Mik's forehead. "Trust me," I whisper the reminder. I know deep down she trusts me. Deep down inside her, in that pit of memories she's refusing to relive, she trusts me. She just needs to remember how she feels about me, remember that she loves me.

My arm snakes around her waist as the elevator dings, alerting us that we've arrived. "You can't come in with me," I tell her. "But I had Beckett meet us here, so he'll sit with you."

Beckett is there when we exit the elevator, waiting for us. I trust him with my life and there are only a few people who fall into that category. He smiles when he sees us, tossing Mik a reassuring grin. I think she's the most comfortable with him out of all my friends, and I know waiting outside while I recount the moments of her sister's death just out of her reach is going to hurt, so she might as well be comfortable.

I leave her in the waiting room with Beckett while David leads me into the office where the deposition will take place. The district attorney is already there, a man who's vying for me to take this to trial. I think he gets his rocks off on sentencing bad guys to life sentences, and he's probably secretly wishing for the death penalty.

He's not alone.

I've tried to avoid everything since the video came out and all of the accusations followed. Every platform is loaded with details of the charges and pictures of me with metal handcuffs slapped across my wrists.

Anyone who hears the story is ready to sentence me to death. Hell, they would lock me up if they could. The comments are a shitshow of name calling and lies. Everyone thinks they know the story, but there were only three people there that night.

One is dead.

One has no memories.

And the weight of the truth rests on me.

I rub a hand over my jaw and try to relax my shoulders, preventing myself from getting worked up. No one knows what happened that night.

Still, I'm anxious, nervous that this whole façade is going to crumble around me.

The conference room we meet in is large, way more space than is needed for the few people here. David directs me to a seat on one side of the table, next to him. The court reporter sits at the head of the table with her keyboard, and David's associates pile in behind me. I take a deep breath, letting the air fill my lungs before I exhale slowly.

The DA is on the other side of the table with his associate, who is working on setting up the camera that will record my words for perpetuity.

Inhale.

Exhale.

I breathe deeply and clasp my hands together, letting them rest on the table in front of me as I watch them ready themselves. DA Miller removes a stack of papers from a thin manila folder and shuffles through them, the actions ruffling the anxiety sitting in my gut.

He lifts his bearded face, locking his gaze with mine, and gives me a brief smile. "So, Mr. Bancroft…" He trails off. He's trying to make me uneasy, draw this out and make me slip. David spent a whole day lecturing me on the tricks that the DA will use to catch me in a lie.

"Where were you on the night of October 31st, 2019?" he asks, his eyes flickering back to mine and holding my gaze.

I swallow the lump building up in my throat. "I was at my parents' home. They were having their annual Halloween party that night."

He nods his head and hums under his breath. "Who all was there?" he asks, his voice stern and serious, asking the questions with no emotion.

"There were a bunch of people," I say. "I can't possibly name them all."

"Your mother said it was a small affair, close friends," he shoots back at me.

I chuckle. "My mother thinks a few hundred people at her house is a small affair," I tell him. "We have differing opinions on what a small party is."

"Okay." He draws the word out. "So tell me then, how many is small to you?"

I nod, mentally trying to tally the people who were there that night. "I think about fifty people, maybe. My family, obviously," I say. "Then the Radcliffes, the Wolfes, and the Monroes, plus all of their kids. And my fiancé, Mikaela."

He gives me an encouraging nod. "When did Auden Wilder show up?" he asks.

I close my eyes for a minute, letting the memory of Auden coming through the door float back to the top of my head. "It was late," I tell him. "Maybe after midnight. I'm not sure. We had all been drinking."

"And where was Mikaela when her sister got there?" The question pops from his lips quickly, one after another, with no space between.

"She was with me. We both saw Auden come through the front door. She was crying. Something had upset her. Mikaela and I both went over to check on her."

"Would you say you were close with your fiancé's younger sister?" There's a menacing look on his face, like he's trying to catch me with this question.

The gossip is filled with theories that there was something happening between Auden and I, that we were hiding a relationship from Mik. "She was like a little sister to me." I shrug. "But I was never really with her without Mik there."

"How often did you spend time with her?" he asks, still trying to trap me, to prove something.

"What are you getting at here?" David growls from his spot next to me.

He shrugs nonchalantly. "Just trying to set the scene."

"I don't know," I answer. "Mik and I were together for two years before that night. I saw Auden lots of times."

"And when you saw her, what were you doing?"

David scoffs at the question, but I answer it. "Mik drove her around a lot. She was in a lot of activities, so I would tag along. If she was home when Mik and I were hanging out, we would let her watch a movie with us, stuff like that."

DA Miller nods his head, flipping through the papers in front of him. "So back to that night, Auden comes into your house crying. Why was she upset?"

The mystery even I don't know. I shake my head. "I'm not sure," I tell him. "We never found out."

"Why?" he asks coldly.

"Mik was drunk. She could barely stand up, so I took her to lay down, and when I came back, I saw Auden leaving through the back. I went to follow her, but she got there before I could..." I wipe a hand over my face, my heart racing as I tell this story, this lie. "She jumped before I could get to her."

"So that's it?" he asks. "She shows up and immediately goes and jumps off a cliff in your backyard without another word?"

"Maybe she liked the view." I give him a half smile.

"Why would she do that? And if she truly just wanted to commit suicide, why would she go to your house?"

I shrug my shoulders involuntarily. "She knew about the cliff. She had been on our property before. I don't know why she would have chosen that."

"I think you do, Mr. Bancroft," he shoots back at me, whipping a sheet of paper from the folder and turning it toward David and me. "The forensics report shows from the angle she hit the ground she had to have been pushed. There is no way Auden Wilder jumped off that cliff, so are you sure that's the story you want to stick with?" A bead of sweat rolls down his face. I think he has himself all worked up from berating me.

"Yes," I answer, keeping my voice steady. "That's the truth. She jumped."

"And you're the only one who saw her, hmm?" he questions me.

"Yes," I say again, confidently. "I watched Auden Wilder jump off the cliff."

10

mik

Halloween Night - One Year Earlier

"Mikaela." I hear Edward's deep rumble from behind me. "I was wondering when you were going to get here." A smile is stretched across his lips when I turn to face him.

Noah's father looks downright sinister. He wears a black tux, perfectly tailored and wrinkle-free. From the neck down, he looks every bit his charming self, but on the crown of his head rests a black mask with grooves and creases, making his face look distorted. The top of the mask stretches out into two large ram horns. In his hand, he holds a matte black pitchfork, long enough that the bottom rests on the ground when he stands.

"The devil?" I ask, looking over his perverse form.

Edward gives me a toothy grin. "Yes," he says, a wicked gleam in his eyes. Noah's dad is unlike my own in many ways, money only being one of them. It's funny when I think about how they work together, a man as confident and commanding as Edward working with a former artist turned businessman like my father.

"Fitting." Noah chuckles under his breath.

"Ah, but this is the devil's night, so it's only fitting that he rules over this party, hmm?" The grin is still plastered on his face while he talks. "Don't you agree?" His deep brown eyes move to mine. "My dark angel?" He reaches forward, stroking a hand against my wings.

I bark out a laugh. "Very fitting." I smile.

"All right, Dad, that's enough." Noah chuckles. "Besides, Mik needs a drink." He tugs on my hand, pulling me away from his father.

"Bye, Mr. Bancroft." I smile as I begin to follow Noah. "Talk to you later." I try my best to sound polite as Noah drags me away. The last thing I need is for his father to hate me. I already know I don't fit in here, in this crowd. The only thing I have going for me is that for some reason, Noah's parents like me.

"I have something for you." Noah leads me away from the other partygoers, toward the French doors at the back of the house. "Let's get some air." He pushes open the doors, pulling us out into the crisp October air.

The trees have already turned, the leaves coating them with shades of orange and red. The Bancroft backyard is completely cleared of them. I'm sure they had someone picking them up as they fell.

The backyard is its own Halloween wonderland. Decorated with string lights hung from the trellis, creating a cozy atmosphere that contradicts with the fake skulls and vases of black roses scattered around the area. Everywhere I look, every corner is decorated with black and muted oranges, roses, and skulls.

The creepy aesthetic has chills running up my arms. I love everything about it.

"You're not dressed up," I say to Noah, once we're outside and I see him fully. He's attractive as always, but his costume is nothing but a simple t-shirt and fitted jeans.

He runs a hand through his dark hair and gives me a quick smile. "Yeah, I guess I just wanted to be myself tonight." He pauses, sucking in a breath of air. "Can we go to our spot?"

It's freezing outside, even for late October, and I rub my hands over my bare arms. "Sure," I tell him.

He takes my hand, leading me back toward our spot. The cliff is the first place Noah took me, the spot he showed me that first time we met. We trek to the back of the property, where the cliff is overlooking the dark water. The moon is bright, tinted with an orange glow as it sits above the water's surface, casting its lights over the lake.

It's beautiful, and fitting for Halloween.

We come here often, whenever we're at his parents' house, and each time I'm stunned by the beauty of this view.

Noah looks nervous, shifting his weight from side to side as we look out at the water.

"Mik," he finally says, running a hand through his hair and pausing to scratch the back of his neck. "I want to ask you something."

"Okay." I smile hesitantly. "Why are you being weird?" It's out of the norm for Noah; he's normally cool and collected. He doesn't sweat about anything, but the man in front of me is definitely nervous about something.

He exhales a rush of air and then drops to one knee. "Mikaela Wilder," he starts. "I know we're young, but I really love you, and I want to spend the rest of my life with you. I like the way I feel when I'm with you. I love seeing you laugh and grow. I love everything about you, Mikaela, and I want every day with you. I want all your love and all your pain. I want everything you have to give. Mik, will you marry me?"

He looks up at me with glossy eyes as he pulls a small velvet box from his pocket, opening it up in front of me. My heart is racing, watching the scene unfold. I'm only nineteen years old, and even though I know I want to spend my life with Noah, I'm shocked. We've talked about marriage, but not this soon.

"Noah," I whisper, not sure what words to say.

The ring in the box in front of me is huge, a large sparkling diamond that looks like it might be the price of a house.

"Say yes, Mik," he says.

"I-" I stutter, still not finding the words.

"Don't overthink this," he adds. "If you love me, say yes and we'll figure everything else out."

I do love him. The small word slips from my lips, and I let him slide the ring onto my finger. I hold my hand out under the moonlight and admire my new rock.

"I love you," he whispers, pressing kisses to the base of my neck.

This is right, I think. This is how it's supposed to be.

Present

My anxiety is through the roof when we finally get back to Noah's house. I need to get away from him, from everybody. My skin feels like it's on fire, my brain racing.

Everything feels worse, heavy, and difficult to understand.

"Mik." I hear Noah's voice call out after me, but I ignore

him. My feet lead me to the stairs and away from him as fast as I can.

I slam the bedroom door behind me, pressing my back against it and melt to the floor. A sob wracks its way through my body, growing from my stomach until I'm heaving, with tears racing down my cheeks.

I haven't cried in a while.

Not about Auden, not about anything.

I've turned myself into a rock. Unfeeling, letting everything roll off of me. If I'm numb, I can't feel the pain. I can't be hurt.

It's better that way, I think.

But Noah split me back open, exposed me to all the feelings and pain I've been hiding from and now everything is attacking me at once. My lungs burn, my heart aches. My whole being is rocked and now that the floodgates have opened, I'm sure I'll never be able to close them back up again.

"Mik." I hear Noah's voice as I feel the reverberations of his knock through the door.

I don't open the door, don't respond to him. Instead, I continue sobbing on the other side, separated from him. His scent lingers in this room though and everything in this house reminds me of him. Even the divider between us can't give me enough space.

"Mik, I can practically hear your head spinning in there," he says through the door, his voice sounding more pained now. "Please, let me in."

The plea feels like it's for more than just letting him into this room. He wants back in my heart, my soul. I don't know if I can do this. I don't know if I can give up everything for him.

I feel another sob wrack my chest, my breathing uneven, as I only suck in a breath between every burst of tears.

"Fuck," Noah growls before pounding his fist on the door, shaking the frame and me along with it.

I hear him move, his steps creaking on the wooden floor as he walks away from the door. Finally, a bit of peace. But it's not long before he's back, shoving something in the lock and pushing the door open, invading my space.

He leans down, hovering over me, taking an assessment of my disheveled appearance before he scoops me up in his arms and carries me to the bed. Laying me down, he curls up next to me with his arms wrapped tightly around me. He holds me as I cry and doesn't let me go until I fall asleep from the exhaustion.

I DON'T KNOW how long I sleep before I feel Noah stir next to me. He shifts, moving away from me and dangling his legs off the bed.

"Hello?" he nearly growls into the speaker of his phone. "Fuck, let 'em through."

It takes me a moment to adjust myself to the world again. There's a haze hanging over me from all the crying. My face feels puffy, my eyes feel sore. My head aches, a constant pounding in my temples.

"What's going on?" I mumble groggily. I wipe the back of my hand across my eyes, probably smearing the makeup I never removed in the process. Noah looks agitated, running his hand through his hair as he sits on the edge of the bed, tucking the cell phone into the pocket of the dress pants he still wears.

"Baby." Noah leans in, fists planted on the mattress, but his voice is as sweet as honey. "I need you to get up, okay?"

His words take a minute to process in my groggy brain. "What's going on?" I repeat.

One hand comes forward, brushing my hair out of my eyes before cupping my face in his palm. "I need you to remember that you trust me, okay?" His dark eyes hold mine, waiting for the answer.

"Okay," I whisper, still half-asleep and unsure about whatever he's talking about.

He gives me a soft smile before leaning in to press a kiss to my forehead. My legs lead me from the bed. I'm sure I look like a mess, tangled hair, smeared makeup, wrinkled dress. Noah doesn't say anything, only reaches forward, wiping the smeared mascara from under my eyes before leading me out of the room.

He doesn't speak again until we're almost at the front door. With his hand on the knob, he turns back to face me. "Your parents are here."

I freeze in my tracks, taking in the words, but before I have a chance to fully respond, the door is opened and my parents come rushing in.

My mom is a whirlwind of frantic energy. She grabs my shoulders, running her hands over me as if she's checking for damage. "Are you okay?" she asks. Her eyes are glossy, holding back tears.

My father is right behind her, looking me over, watching for any signs that something is amiss. "Mikaela." His voice shakes when he speaks my name. "Are you okay?"

They're both staring at me with wide eyes, waiting for a response, but my voice isn't working. I can't gather the words to say anything to them. I feel like a traitor, like I abandoned them for the other side. In some ways I did...

"She's fine." Noah's voice sounds, and my eyes find him standing behind us by the front door, arms across his chest.

My father whips around faster than I can realize, marching toward Noah with a finger pointed. "You little shit," he growls.

Noah holds his hands up defensively. "She wants to be here, Judah. It's her choice."

Instantly, all sets of eyes turn back to me. "Mikaela," my mother says softly. "What's going on?"

My eyes flick from my mom to my dad before landing on Noah. He gives me a slight nod, the okay signal to talk. But the words he wants me to say are going to hurt. That much I know.

"I'm fine." My voice is hoarse, sounding broken.

My father visibly winces and a single tear rolls down my mother's cheek. My stomach churns at the thought of how this is hurting them, ripping them apart.

They've been convinced it was Noah since that morning when I called them. When they woke up to both of their daughters missing from their beds.

She's gone, Mom.

Those were the words I said that morning, when I rose out of my haze to find out my sister jumped off the cliff. The police had come and gone all while I was too fucked up to even move.

To even know my sister was there at all.

She was supposed to be at another party, where I dropped her off. I watched her walk into that house and give me a wave before I drove away. Yet somehow, she ended up miles away at the Bancroft estate and dead within hours.

I tried to run out to the cliff after Noah told me the news. I can still feel the way his arms latched around my waist, fingers gripping into my skin while I screamed and cried for her.

If he would have let me go, I would have followed her over, something I've thought about every day for the last year.

Mom. Dad. Noah. I repeat their names as a mantra, the

only thing that keeps me clinging to life when I'd much rather end it. If I can't stay alive for myself, I'll do it for them. Even Noah.

Pain sears through my chest, hitting me like a ton of bricks. I can barely breathe through it, but I grit my teeth and try to face my parents.

"I want to be here," I whisper, dropping my gaze to avoid seeing their faces when they hear the words.

"What the fuck did you do to her?" my father shouts at Noah. His eyes are nearly black, dark with rage, and he raises his fists as if he's going to hit him.

"Nothing," Noah snarls back, unleashing his own anger.

My mother spins around, widening her arms and blocking me from the men as if I'm too fragile to see this. Parents always treat their firstborns like delicate flowers, fragile and easy to break. I push her arm out of the way.

"You fucking did something to her. What did you do?" My father is screaming now. I can see little drops of saliva leave his mouth, landing on Noah's face.

My father's not a big man. The only thing he has on Noah is age, and that won't help him in a fight. His slim frame is the same height as Noah's, but his growl seems louder, harsher.

It must be the pain of losing Auden that fuels him now, ignites a fire. It's funny that he walked through life like it was pointless, drinking away his sorrows when she was alive, and now that she's dead, he has some sort of purpose.

Grief is a greater fuel than money could ever be.

"Judah, calm the fuck down," Noah tells him, a slight edge to his voice. "Mikaela's fine. Do you really think I would hurt her?'

I push past my mother, grabbing my father's arms and pulling him away from Noah. He lets me, or else I don't think I would have been successful.

"Dad," I whimper, pushing my body to his, wrapping my arms around him. "I'm sorry." Tears drip down from my eyes as I hug him.

His body tenses before it relaxes, and he wraps his own arms around me. "It's okay," he whispers. "It's okay, Mikaela. I'm not mad at you."

"I fucked up," I cry, all the pain and sorrow coming back to me again. "I should have protected her, but I can't even remember what happened."

I feel my mother come up behind me, wrapping her arms around me and joining our hug. "Shh," she whispers. "Everything's okay."

Once I calm down, I sit wrapped in a blanket on the couch next to my father while my mother makes tea in the kitchen. Noah stands in the corner like a statue with his arms crossed over his chest. He's trying to give us space to grieve as a family, but he also wants to see what I'll do, what I'll say.

"I'm fine, really," I say, tugging the blanket tighter around me. "You don't need to stay."

"Nonsense," my father says to me, but his eyes stay trained on Noah. "We'll stay."

My mother shuffles back into the kitchen with two mugs of tea in her hand. "Drink this," she says, shoving one into my hands, the warm mug permeating my skin, thawing me. She sits down next to me on the leather couch in Noah's living room, pressing out the skirt of her dress nervously. She watches me, her matching green eyes filled with sadness. "We're just worried," she says gravely.

"I know," I tell her softly. "I swear, I'm okay."

"I just"—she wrings her hands together—"we saw pictures. You went to the deposition today…" Her eyes are watery again, and I can tell she's trying her best to ask me without getting angry, without yelling. "Do you…" She trails off. "Do you remember what happened?" She looks at me hopefully.

My memory has been a sore subject with everyone. I was there. I should know what happened. I should remember seeing my sister, remember her crying. I should have been there for her.

I was so drunk, so far gone. I can't even remember the drinks, how many I had, or what they were.

Everything from that night is a dark pit, buried deep beneath the ground's surface and then blurred, out of focus.

There are pieces, tiny details. Muted orange, black roses —but everything is just fragments. Broken pieces that I can't put back together again.

"No," I whisper.

She nods her head, turning from me slowly. All the hope is draining from her face.

"I'm sorry," I say again, not able to say those words enough, the tears threatening to work their way back to the surface. "I've tried. I just... can't."

"Shh," she whispers, bringing her hands to wrap around my arm, pulling me close to her. "It's okay."

"Mik." My father speaks now, leaning forward to place each of his elbows on his knees. He looks bad, disheveled. Like he hasn't been sleeping. His clothes are slightly wrinkled, his hair is graying. "You know better than any of us what happened that night. Somewhere in there, you know. If you trust him, if you want to stay here, I can't stop you." He pauses, sighing heavily. "I think he's dangerous." His eyes flicker up to meet Noah's. "I can't promise that we'll stop. I'll fight until my last breath to put him behind bars. I'm not going to force you out of here." He rises, dusting off his khakis. "But I hope you'll come with me."

He gestures for my mother to follow him, and I can feel

her tense. She studies me again, her eyes pleading with me, wanting me to follow.

But I won't.

Because even without looking at him, I can feel Noah's eyes on me from the corner of the room and the thought of leaving him tears at something in me. It shouldn't; I owe him nothing.

I'm not sure what he would do if I left. I don't know what he has over me. I want to pretend I'm afraid for my life, just to have an excuse. But I'm not sure I even believe that he would hurt me.

"I'll stay," I whisper, avoiding their eyes once again tonight.

My mother kisses my cheek wordlessly, rising from the couch to join my father. They leave quickly and quietly, as if they'd never even been here.

Noah's on me in seconds, kissing my head, my cheeks, my lips. "Good job, baby girl," he murmurs, and I feel like I'm being rewarded the same way you would a trained dog.

Sit. Stay. *Good job, baby girl.*

11

noah

Three Years Earlier

Being with Mik is intoxicating.

I watch her with a euphoric amazement. She dances next to Pax, the grumpiest of all of us, with the biggest smile spread across her face. Pax, on the other hand, is not amused.

She's the only one in this shitty bar dancing. She's also the one who suggested this dump. I think she wanted to see how out of place the four of us would look in this shitty college town bar.

But she's happy, that's clear.

Not even twenty-one yet, she brings a cup of Natty Light to her lips—a plastic cup because that's what this dive bar serves their drinks in.

Beckett chuckles next to me, watching the scene unfold. Mik uses the cup as a microphone while she mouths the words of whatever bubblegum pop song blares through the speakers.

She's electric. Being with her sends a spark through my

body, consuming me. I'm like an addict when I'm with her, obsessed with her. My eyes can't stop watching her every move.

Dancing her way over to me, she sways her hips in the tight ripped skinny jeans that are plastered to her body. She wears a cropped hoodie and there's about an inch of her stomach exposed between her hoodie and jeans, giving me a glimpse of her smooth skin beneath the clothes.

Green eyes find me, watching my gaze trail over her. She stalks closer, hooking a leg around me so she's hovering over me, her tits perfectly level with my head. Her body moves with the music and her eyes drop down to lock with mine.

Instinctively, my hands move to her waist, gripping her hips. A quick rhythm is beating in my chest, all of my senses heightened from being around her. She's like a drug, slipping me into a blissful state where everything feels better.

All of the shit in my life, all the issues with my family, the business, the obligations—everything slips away when I'm with her.

Each of us have our vices. Beckett gets high to sink away from his mind. Vaughn relies on booze. And Pax, well, Pax gets his thrills in other, more painful ways.

I use her.

My safe haven, my heart. She dulls the ache, chases away the monsters, steadies me. I don't even think she realizes. I don't think she knows what she does to me.

Her head drops down to kiss me slowly. "You're stuck in your head." She taps my forehead to illustrate her point. "What are you thinking about?" she asks, her lips turned up into a smile.

"You," I tell her. That's the truth. She runs through my mind constantly.

"Yeah?" She grins.

"Yeah, baby, always you."

When I take her home later, she drops to her knees for me, a devilish smile tugging at her lips as she frees my cock from my jeans. When it's just us behind closed doors, she turns into a slut for me, taking my cock and running her tongue from base to tip. She keeps her eyes trained on mine, watching how her every move brings me closer to the edge.

It's sloppy the way she lathers me with her saliva as she works her hand along my length and sucks on the tip. I want to come that way, cover her in my release, but I want to fuck her even more than that.

Mik squeals as I pull her up to her feet before pushing her back onto my bed and freeing her of the tight skinny jeans. I slap her ass and in response, and she pushes it farther out for me. She's always liked sex with a little bite, a bit of pain to take the edge off. Blonde hair flips over her shoulder and she looks back at me, a challenging smirk lining her lips.

"Harder," she goads me, and something flares in my chest, a lust I can't explain. A carnal need to have this girl.

I bring my open palm down on her ass again, slapping against the cotton material of her panties. She hisses out a small yelp, but I know she likes it. And if she doesn't, she'll safeword out.

"Fuck me, Noah," she moans the words, and my already stiff cock aches at the sound.

She doesn't need to ask me again. I tug down her panties and she arches her back for me, giving me unlimited access to her sweet cunt.

And when I thrust into her, we both moan in ecstasy, our bodies coming together in perfect harmony. My hand reaches forward, fingers wrapping around the column of her throat. My girl loves to be choked while I fuck her, shaking as she fights to breathe, her body overcome with pleasure.

Her pussy turns into a vice, squeezing my cock as she comes, and I follow her over that cliff. We finish together before collapsing onto the bed, breathless and sticky with cum and sweat, but when I look over at her, she's smiling, completely sated and happy as fuck.

I can't get enough of her.

Present

Mik squirms beneath me, breaking herself out of my grasp and pushing me off her in one fluid motion. The look on her face sends daggers through my heart.

Sadness.

Confusion.

Pain.

So much fucking pain. All the emotions play on her features while she backs away from me, sucking in ragged breaths.

"What did I just do?" The question leaves her lips in a broken cry. I see the glistening of tears pooling above her lower lash line. She has her back against the living room wall next to the fireplace, one hand on her chest, the other extended to ward me off.

"What you had to do, baby," I coo, slowly approaching her with both of my hands extended. I'm not a threat to her right now, and I need her to see that.

I need her to realize that we're in this together. We're a fucking team, always have been. She can't run from this, hide from me.

But she's still panting, dragging in air like she can't get enough.

She's cracking. I can see it happening right in front of me. Everything about her is falling to pieces and she can barely stand while it happens. I can practically feel the spiral in her head, dragging her back down into the depths of her sorrow.

I keep moving closer to her, but she's on edge. Hastily, she grabs the poker below the mantle before I can even grasp what she's doing. She extends the long, jagged stick to me, holding me off with the weapon.

"What is going on?" Her voice cracks on the last word, another fracture showing.

I tried to protect her from this. Really, I did. I tried to give her space, let her live without me.

But we just don't work like that.

"Mik," I murmur. "Come on, baby."

"Don't baby me," she growls, thrusting the poker forward. "You're making me fucking crazy, Noah. Do you realize that?" she huffs, bringing one hand up to her face to wipe away the stray tears. "I'm trying to trust you, I am, but you need to tell me what the fuck is going on!" she screams now.

Luckily for us, there are no houses close enough to hear her, so she can yell out all she fucking wants here. No one is going to come save her here. It's just us now. Caught in the fists of truth surrounding us.

"Mik," I try again, but she just jabs the poker forward.

"Don't speak unless the truth is coming out of your mouth!"

"And then what?" I growl. "You think that you'll just magically feel better then? That if you know all the bloody details you can't remember that everything will be okay? It won't, Mik. Don't be fucking naive. Because I know the truth, baby girl, and I'm just as fucking broken as you are."

She chokes on another sob, her eyes closing with a wince and the arm holding the poker sags. It gives me an opportunity to rush forward, ripping the poker from her limp arm and tossing it, letting it clatter against the hardwood floors. I grab her, wrapping my arms tightly around her in a vice she can't escape.

"Do you know what this has been like for me? Hmm?" I growl into her ear. "What it's like to not be able to leave my house without a news van tailing me? To have lies spread about me all over the fucking news? Have you thought for a second what this is like for me, or have you been too holed up in your head, only thinking about your damn self?"

Her head rears back and her green eyes find me. They're filled with hurt, pain at my words. "You think you're the victim here?" she sneers.

"Yeah, baby. The way I see it, I'm the one looking at the fucking death penalty."

A rough laugh escapes her though, like this is some kind of funny joke. "You'll never go to prison. You and I both know that." She chuckles, a sinister, broken sound. "You don't even need me here for that. I'm just your rehabilitation for the press, right? Just a way to make you look like you're not a monster? Because we both know Edward Bancroft isn't about to let his only son go to prison, and he has the connections to make that happen."

There's my girl.

Smart. Perceptive. Clever.

I grin. "You're not wrong, but it doesn't change anything."

"Why?" she barks.

"Really, Mik? Because I fucking want you here. Because you're fucking mine." I feel her flinch in my arms at the roughness of my words, but it doesn't stop me. She needs to hear this, every last word.

I drag her with me to the credenza against the other wall, making her yelp at the tightness of my grip. Our bodies are flush against each other, hers pinned between mine and the piece of furniture. I use one hand to open the top drawer, pulling a bit of rope I have stored there.

I back up just enough to give her some space to move.

"Turn around," I tell her.

She does. For some reason, she fucking listens to me. She whips her head back toward me, watching me through a veil of blonde hair. "What are you doing?"

I grab her wrists, pinning them together behind her back while I wrap the rope around, securing them tightly together. "Do you know what happens when you get arrested, Mikaela?" I taunt. "It's fucking humiliating, baby girl. Having metal handcuffs wrapped around my fucking wrists." I tug on her newly secured hands for effect.

A whimper leaves her lips, but no words, nothing else. "Then," I continue. "The fucking perp walk. Can you imagine it? Being escorted from your house with a shit ton of police?" I pull her back into my chest and then spin us around, pushing her forward so she starts to walk. "I want you to picture it, baby girl, while I walk you upstairs." I push her forward again, leading her toward the stairs and making her march up ahead of me.

I can practically feel the nervous energy radiating from her, but it doesn't stop me.

It only makes me want this more.

I want her to break for me.

Surrender to me.

I want her to be fucking mine again, all of her.

She tosses a look over her shoulder at me as we enter the

bedroom. "Noah," she breathes, but it's ragged and husky. I know she wants this as much as I do.

"You know what they do next? Push you into a police car, take you to the fucking station, fingerprints, mug shots. Nobody looks good in a mug shot, baby."

I push her toward the bed. "Get on your knees, baby girl," I tell her, and she complies, letting me lift her up enough so she can put her knees on the bed. She shimmies forward, so she's not on the edge, and waits for me.

"Then they toss you in a cell with a bunch of other criminals." I reach forward, lifting the bottom of the navy-blue dress up so it's around her waist, giving me a full view of her round ass in her white lacy panties. She's a beautiful fucking sight, creamy skin and white lace on top of the black silk sheets.

She's an angel, waiting to be engulfed in the darkness.

"Do you think I'm a criminal? Do you think I'm the bad guy here, baby?" I circle around the bed so I'm standing before her. I reach for the buttons of the dress, slowly undoing each one while she watches me. "Do you?"

She doesn't answer, her lips are pressed together in a thin line, but her eyes are glued to everything I do and say.

With all of the buttons undone, she's exposed to me. Her white bra matches the panties and lifts her perfect tits, putting them on display for me. The dress hangs off her shoulders, bunching around the makeshift handcuffs.

I rub my fingers down her face, feeling her smooth skin. She leans into it, her eyes drifting closed for a moment. "Did you like being without me?" I question.

Her green eyes shoot open and move to meet mine. "No," she breathes. "I fucking loved it."

"Liar," I sneer.

"Takes one to know one." She smiles at me, a fucking wide grin, but it only makes me want her more.

"Yeah, baby, we're both liars." I lean forward, whispering the words in her ear with a growl. "I tried to let you go," I whisper. "But I didn't like it very much, and I don't think you did either."

I trace her lips with my thumb, pulling down her lower one a bit and making her gasp. I can tell she's on edge, thighs clenched, pupils dilated.

"But we both know you want this as much as I do." This time she doesn't respond, just holds eye contact with me. "Ask me, baby girl, ask me for all the dirty things you want me to do to you."

A grimace marks her features. She doesn't want to beg me tonight, doesn't want to give into this thing between us. I lean back, standing from the bed and backing away. "Nothing happens unless you ask for it."

Her mouth twists into a frown as she watches me back up. "Okay," she whispers. "Fuck me, Noah."

"Do better," I tell her, crossing my arms over my chest. "I'll wait."

A rush of air burst from her lips in a huff. "Please. Please, Noah, fuck me."

I don't move a muscle, my eyes training on her, waiting for her to say more, to really give herself over to me.

"I want to feel you," she continues, taking a deep inhale. "I want to feel you inside me again." Her eyes flash up to mine, and I feel that connection, that burst of energy between us.

I rush forward, capturing her head in my hands and pressing my mouth to her. We devour each other like we've been deprived, like our lives depend on each other. And maybe they do.

Maybe we're nothing alone, but together we're fucking unstoppable.

I reach down, pushing her panties aside and slipping a

finger through her folds. She's already wet for me, ready. She moans against my mouth while I draw lazy circles on her clit.

"Please," she begs again, and it's fucking music to my ears. I love hearing her beg and moan. I live for every sound that leaves those plump lips.

Tugging her bottom lip between my teeth, I give her a nip, just enough to draw a little blood. The metallic copper fills my mouth, giving me a better taste of her.

I pull back, and in one fluid motion, I'm yanking off my pants and boxers, tossing them off the bed. I spin her around so I can push her forward, letting her face hit the silk sheets.

"Open your legs," I tell her as I nudge them apart, giving me access to her sweet pussy.

I waste no time diving into her cunt, making her cry out beneath me.

Her sounds are beautiful, and for a moment, everything feels right again. Deep inside her, making her moan and beg for me. Every noise is an ode to me.

I want her beside me every moment of every damn day.

She can't hide from me.

And one day, when the truth hunts her down, I'll be here to soften the blow.

12

mik

Halloween Night - One Year Earlier

I'm giggling when we return to the party. All doubts have drifted away, my mind solely focused on the happiness in front of me.

It feels weird to be this happy, a strange feeling for me almost, but I'm on fire right now, electrified with this happiness flowing through me. Noah looks just as happy, a grin spreading across his lips. He looks at me every few seconds, as if he is checking to make sure that same grin is plastered across my face.

It is.

Every damn time.

My mother will cry tears of joy when she finds out about this engagement. She'll have my wedding dress picked out by Monday. She's probably been planning my wedding day since the day I was born. She adores Noah, finds him charming. She'll be grateful that it's him who put a ring on my finger, and not any of my exes.

She might be shallow, might think that money equates to

how good a person is, but I won't be the one to argue this with her. She can think whatever she wants about Noah, as long as she likes him.

My father, on the other hand, will probably be skeptical. He has been since the first date we went on. He was shocked when he learned his boss's son had asked me out. I think he wanted to keep us disconnected from his work life, wanted to keep the two things as separate as possible, and our relationship kind of messed that up.

He treated the Bancrofts as if they were a secret family, one he didn't want the first family to know about. It was strange, because when he was with Edward, they acted like they were best friends. You would have never thought that he was secretly hoping for their children to break up.

Break up might be dramatic, but still, he won't be thrilled about the news of our engagement.

"Dad," Noah calls out to Edward. "I want to make an announcement."

Edward nods his head toward us, giving his silent agreement for Noah to continue on with his announcement.

Noah drags me toward the musicians, asking them to pause the music. The main area of the Bancroft house is filled with party guests. All of the inner circle is here, each couple with their kids, plus a handful of others. Friends, family, significant others.

"Tonight," Noah speaks loud and clear for the group, "I asked Mikaela to marry me." He smiles at me, remembering the moment. "And she said yes."

There's cheering around us, congratulations. I'm being hugged left and right, my hand being pulled, women gawking over the ring.

I catch sight of Edward standing in the back of the room, away from us, but I can still see the slight smile on his face.

Mariam is next to him, but she doesn't look as thrilled. Instead, she looks nervous. Scared even.

It's a whirlwind of congratulations before Edward and Mariam come over to us. Edward hands us each a glass of champagne.

"Cheers," he says. "Welcome to the family, Mikaela."

Present

I spend the next few days ignoring Noah, using space as a defense mechanism. I'm trying to hide in my room like a coward, attempting to read a book. I can't focus, though. My mind keeps going back to that afternoon with him, to my hands bound behind my back.

His story, the things he said to me, all of his words keep replaying in my mind.

He wasn't wrong. I never thought about what he was going through, what it was like for him. In my mind, Noah is indestructible. I guess I always imagined him not flinching during the whole arrest, probably chuckling while they slapped the handcuffs on him and stuffed him into the back of a police cruiser.

Was he scared? Nervous? Did the arrest finally break the indestructible Noah Bancroft?

Auden infiltrates my dreams. Images of her looking sad, running from something, or to something, play on repeat. I can see the black drips of her mascara as tears run down her cheeks. I can't place the dream, not sure if it's a memory or my subconscious haunting me.

Noah keeps himself locked in his office. He's still working for his father during this whole ordeal, in between meetings with his lawyer and pre-trial activities. Something only the rich can manage, being on trial and still running a Fortune 500 company.

He must be done now though, because I can hear music coming from downstairs and voices floating through the hall. Soft conversations drawing my attention, telling me the boys must be downstairs.

I pad lightly over to the door to listen closer.

"Mikaela," I hear Beckett call, laughter following after.

"She won't come down." I hear next, this time from Pax.

"Mik!" Beckett calls again.

Beckett probably has weed, and I tell myself that's the only reason I'm going down there. I could use an escape, a reprieve from today. It sucked, so I deserve this, right? I open the door, eliciting a soft creak, and step out into the hallway. I'm wearing a pair of soft pink shorts and an oversized white sweatshirt with my hair twisted into a messy bun on my head. I haven't dressed up since the deposition hearing, opting for comfy clothes instead.

"Yes!" Beckett laughs when he sees me at the top of the stairs, and immediately, he extends a hand toward Pax.

His friend growls as he pulls cash from his back pocket and slaps it in Beckett's hand. "Fuck." He slumps back on the couch, crossing his arms and tossing me a glare.

"Ignore them," Noah says when I falter on the steps. "Come here, baby girl."

I hate the way my core clenches at the sound of his voice. My body betrays me by responding to him so eagerly. I continue my descent, eyes locked on Pax and Beckett. "Were you two betting on me?"

Beckett chuckles. "Pax didn't think I could get you to come downstairs."

The boys are spread out in the living room, Pax and Beckett on the long couch, Vaughn in the chair, and Noah on the loveseat. Each holding a sweating tumbler of hard liquor over ice.

Noah pats the cushion next to him, summoning me over like a dog. I turn to see him over my shoulder, sending him a sharp glare for thinking that would entice me to sit with him. He can't control me. The other day was just a fluke, a lapse in judgment for me.

"Can we smoke?" I ask, turning my head back and addressing Beckett.

He doesn't answer me at first, instead he looks around me and at Noah, waiting for his approval first. "Sure," Noah sighs and Beckett eagerly hops off the couch with a smile plastered to his face.

I resist the urge to say something shitty to them, to express that I don't need Noah's approval to do a damn thing. But I know it won't matter. These men have known each other their entire lives. Their friendship, their brotherhood, means more than my feelings. So I keep my mouth shut, lips pursed.

"You want any, Noah?" he asks, leading me out back, but I don't hear Noah answer, nor do I turn around to see any gestures.

Beckett sits in one of the cushioned chairs out on Noah's back patio and pulls a joint and a lighter from his pocket. "I knew you wouldn't stay upstairs all night." He laughs, flicking the lighter to life and bringing it to the tip of the joint.

The patio is actually pretty nice. This is my first time using it, since I've been too stubborn to do anything but sit in my room. The view looks out into the woods, long stretches of trees blocking everything else from sight. He has neighbors on either side, but there's a lot of land between the houses and a divider made up of trees and greenery.

"Yeah, well, I was bored." I take the joint from his outstretched fingers and inhale deeply.

Vapor burn my lungs before I blow out the trail of smoke, watching it drift away softly. The high buzzes through me, slowly beginning the numbing process. I take another puff immediately. I want to be higher, further away from all the chaos in this house… in my head.

Beckett snatches the joint back. "I know what you're doing, Mik." he says, taking a drag. "You're trying to escape." A stray piece of dark golden hair falls in front of his eyes, and he leans farther back in the chair while he uses a hand to brush it away.

I give him a serious look. "Isn't that what you're doing?"

Beckett is always trying to escape, always getting his hands on whatever drug will get him there, get him out of his head. His father is an asshole, and an utterly terrible person. Malcom Monroe owns the biggest media conglomerate on the East Coast. Monroe Media was home to news outlets, television shows, and more local papers than one could count. He had a history of buying small papers for cheap and liquidating all their assets, leaving employees out of work as quickly as he could legally get away with. And what he couldn't legally get away with, he had Vaughn's father help him with.

He chuckles, tapping the joint in the ashtray. "It's different."

Like hell it is. I collapse in the cushioned chair next to him, sinking into the pillows. "How?" I ask him, because I know it's not different. We're both avoiding something, hiding from it and using any means necessary to keep reality at bay.

"I don't have a whole night of missing memories," he deadpans, his blue eyes focused on me.

I want to laugh, but I know he's not joking. "Do you know what happened?" I ask.

I've been asked this same question on repeat for the last year. Police, therapists, my family—everyone wants to know what happened that night. Why did Auden show up at the Bancroft Estate? Why was she crying? Why was she out there? Did she jump?

But I've never asked anyone else but Noah. For some reason, I know he knows. I know he was there. He should have all the answers, but he keeps them wrapped up, a secret hidden in the depths of his mind.

He keeps asking me to trust him, and I want to, I really do. When I'm with him, I'm reminded of all the good times, everything before my life spiraled out of control. I want to get back there, back to happiness.

My arms begin to lighten, going slack at my sides before Beckett begins to speak. He watches me for a moment before he shakes his head. "I wasn't there." His eyes move away from me as he avoids my gaze, leaning back in the chair and exhaling a cloud of smoke.

"But you were at the party," I retort.

All of the inner circle was there that night. Beckett, Vaughn, Pax, yet I've never asked a single one of them what they know. What they remember from that fateful night.

He brings the joint back up to his lips, taking another long inhale and blowing the smoke out. "Yeah," he tells me. "But not at the cliffs."

I huff, leaning back into my seat again. I have a sudden urge to know the truth, something I thought I had let go of. Now, every inch of my skin is buzzing, begging to know what happened that night. What happened to my sister.

"You should trust him." Beckett says, handing me the joint again.

I release a harsh breath before bringing it back to my

lips. "Why?" I ask as the smoke bursts from my mouth and the burning in my lungs makes me cough for a solid minute before he can speak again.

Beckett sighs next to me, adjusting his position in his seat so he can see me better. "He loves ya, ya know?" He plucks the joint from my fingertips, taking another pull for himself. "He's trying to protect you. Hell, Mikaela, I think he would go to prison if it meant protecting you."

I laugh grimly. "Noah will never go to prison."

"You think that," Beckett counters. "But social media is one hell of a tool. It's harder to hide things these days, and that fucking video is putting Noah under a microscope." He sighs, leaning back again. "If Noah doesn't win over the public, it won't fucking matter if the case gets thrown out. Trial by media, ya know."

Trial by media.

It's funny, I think. When you're a kid, you believe everything is black and white, good and bad. You think all adults know what they're doing and make the right decisions. You have so much faith in the legal system, but that's just not how things work.

There's a reason the Bancrofts built their multi-million-dollar house so close to Washington, D.C.

Power. So much fucking power.

Their influence in politics can make or break someone, they can spin details, trap their opponents. And at their aid are three of the other richest families.

They can get away with almost anything.

But *this*.

This trial might be the death of them.

Because of Twitter, of all things. My parents barely even knew what they were doing; it was one of Auden's friends who filmed the video and helped them get it online.

It was a PR nightmare for the Bancrofts, but the first

step in justice for Auden. They filmed it in her bedroom, my mom holding an old stuffed animal on her lap while tears were running from her eyes.

They told her story.

On Halloween night, Auden Wilder went to a party with friends. Around 11:00 PM, she left the party visibly upset, calling an Uber to take her to the Bancroft Estate where her sister was. Sometime between 11:30 PM and midnight, she was pushed off the cliff at the back of the Bancroft property. No one saw her leaving out the back door, but Noah Bancroft. Bancroft put himself at the scene, saying he saw her jump. There's no way the high school honor student and soccer star jumped off the cliff, and a second forensics analysis proves that the way she hit the ground is inconsistent with jumping. She was pushed, and the only one who saw her was Noah Bancroft.

People couldn't stop watching the video, and it spread like wildfire.

Some just wanted to see an elitist go down, I'm sure, wanted to see the rich and famous be punished for their actions instead of just having everything swept under the rug. Others were moved by my parents, by their tragic loss.

I had begged them not to post the thing, not to go up against the Bancrofts, but they didn't listen.

I don't think they cared after losing Auden. They would rather die, go down fighting, than let everything get swept under the rug. Dad quit his job at Bancroft Co. immediately following Auden's death. They've been living off savings for the past year, taking money out of their retirement. They have no plans to enjoy life anymore. The only thoughts they have revolve around putting Noah behind bars.

And here I am, protecting him.

"Beckett?" I ask softly.

"Yeah, Mik?" His eyes are glassy. He's high now, floating into a happier headspace. I like talking to people like this, like being like this. I'm lighter, my mind is clearer, the constant stream of noise and thoughts in my head is gone. All I hear are the crickets singing from the grass and the ringing of wind chimes in the distance. It's peaceful, for once.

"Do you think Noah did it?" I ask, my voice wavering.

"Nah," he says, eyes locked with mine, watching me. "Noah would never hurt you like that. It was just…" He trails off, looking for the right words. "An unfortunate accident."

13

mik

Noah hasn't moved an inch since I went outside. He's leaning back on the loveseat, one arm slung over the cushions and one ankle crossed over his knee. His dark eyes flicker up when I return, traveling over my frame first, inspecting me.

Sometimes I feel like he's looking for my broken pieces, making sure they're not showing. That the façade is completely intact. I wonder what he thinks when he looks at me like that. Is he tallying up the flaws? Or does he see past my outward appearance, instead gravitating toward my broken soul, wondering how he'll fix what he shattered?

"Feel better?" he asks, the corner of his lip turning up into a smirk.

He's an asshole, sarcastic, villainous.

But looking at him now, I'm reminded of all the reasons I fell in love with him. I can see him clearly, that first day when I met him in the bathroom. Before he took me to the edge of the cliff, got me high, and wormed his way into my life.

"Much." I smile, feeling the nerves in my face light up as I do.

He grins back in response. "Come here, baby girl." This time, I do as he asks and head over to him, sinking into the loveseat next to him and tucking my head into his neck.

He flinches at first, surprised by my sudden obedience and affection. Then, he softens, letting my body sink into his, melding us as one.

"You feeling okay?" he asks, a near whisper directly into my ear.

I feel lighter, even though my conversation with Beckett felt dark. Between the weed and Beckett's advice, I felt more content than I had. Gone are my worries of choosing. Choosing a side, my family or Noah. Beckett didn't think Noah did it, and I trusted Beckett.

At the end of the day, I knew that if he was forced to choose between me or Noah, he would always be loyal to Noah first. But outside, when it was just us with our minds quieter, I felt his sorrow, his compassion. I trust him.

And deep down, I've always trusted Noah.

So I raise my head to meet his gaze. "Yeah," I whisper. "I feel much better."

Soft lips meet the crown of my head, leaving a gentle kiss.

Beckett stumbles in behind me, plopping down on the couch and stretching out his legs. "So, are we all a happy family again?" He laughs.

Noah nudges me. "What do you think, Mik? We good?"

The question is heavy, but it bounces off of me with no hesitation. "Yeah," I answer. "I trust you."

My answer brings a wide grin to Noah's face. He's more than happy with me, looking nearly high himself at my words, like no other sentence could have made him this happy. He leans in, placing a hard kiss on my lips, dragging my bottom lip in between his teeth and biting gently. "Fuck, baby," he moans into my mouth.

He presses his hard body against me, backing me into the couch cushion. Slowly, he drags a hand up the side of my body, trailing his fingertips up my thigh over the curve of my waist. He traces over my abdomen and around my breast, drawing his fingers ever so slowly up to my collarbone, letting them rest there for a moment.

My skin is on fire from his touch, every nerve ending alive and sending electricity through my entire body. Suddenly, I want his touch everywhere. Warmth pools in my lower belly, the need growing stronger. I arch my back, pushing against him and trying to find friction wherever I can get it.

"Do you need something, baby?" he whispers mockingly, one eyebrow pinched up in question.

"Yes," I breathe, the word so quiet I'm not sure if he even hears me.

"Tell me," he demands, always wanting to hear me say it.

"You." I can barely get a full sentence out between the fire rising inside my body and the fog that clouds my brain.

"We have guests, baby girl. Are you gonna let them join?"

I suddenly become aware that the boys are here. I almost forgot about them in my hazy bubble surrounding Noah and me. I look over to them, and three sets of eyes look back at me expectantly. How long have they been listening?

"Well, baby?" Noah questions. He's still running his hand over my body, stopping every so often to circle his thumb over my nipples, teasing them as they strain beneath the fabric of my shirt.

It's not the first time we've done this, shared with his friends. A part of me knows it's dirty and wrong, a little fucked up. But another part of me loves it. The way their eyes are glued to me, I watch as Vaughn's tongue traces the line of his bottom lip.

"Yes," I whisper. I'm so hot right now, my body on fire with need. I need to feel them, all of them.

It feels like it happens quickly. As soon as the word leaves my lips, the boys are surrounding me, one on every side. Hands trace over my body. My shoulders, my back, my tits, my thighs—everything is being touched, massaged, pinched.

I'm straddled on Noah's lap, and his head is in the crook of my neck, kissing me all over, sending chills down my spine. "Do you like this, baby? You like having everyone's hands on you?" Noah sneers.

"Yes," I answer with a shallow breath. I love it, having all of the attention, all of their hands exploring every inch of me. But I want more. I want them lower.

"You're needy for them. Aren't you, baby?" he taunts.

My body responds to him before I can. My breath hitches, my thighs shake, and I can feel myself grinding on Noah, searching for any amount of friction. Anything to get me there.

"Say it," he orders, his voice colder.

Noah's a controlling asshole, demanding and dominant. Only every once in a while does he share like this, and only with his brothers, and only on his terms.

"I want them," I moan, and his mouth comes to mine, kissing me roughly. He pulls back and I feel the other hands start to leave me, eliciting a whimper. Noah's hands come to me instead, pulling the hoodie off of me, tossing it to the floor in a heap of fabric.

I'm braless underneath, exposed to them without the protection of my hoodie.

"Fucking beautiful," Noah breathes, and the words penetrate my skin, making me feel alive and powerful. "Up," he demands. "I want these off," he tells me, snapping the waistband of my shorts.

I stand quickly, letting him slip the shorts and my panties down my legs. He leans in to kiss me, simultaneously bringing his hand to my pussy, nudging me open. I widen my stance for him, giving him the space he needs.

He slips a finger through my folds, gathering my wetness and circling it around my clit. A moan escapes my lips as soon as he touches me. All of the touching, the dirty words have me worked up and needing a release.

"Please," I beg.

"Not yet," he says, pulling away from me quickly and leaving me empty. He sits back down on the loveseat and pats his leg. "I want you to sit here, baby girl. I want you to show my brothers your pretty pussy."

I do as he says, sitting on his lap and spreading my legs for him. His fingers come back to me, slipping one through my slit and back up to my clit, swirling my wetness around the bundle of nerves.

"Do you want Beckett's fingers in your cunt, baby?" he growls, and instinctively, I nod, because I do. I want to feel more.

Beckett wastes no time, dropping to his knees on the hard floor and coming closer to me. He spreads my lips, dipping a single finger into me, slowly finding a rhythm.

Pax and Vaughn are on either side of me now. I feel Pax's warm tattooed hand come to my tit, palming me and pinching my nipple. Vaughn's hands are rubbing my opposite arm, his fingers trailing up to my collarbone, then my jawline.

There's so much sensation, so many things to feel. The warmth in my stomach is expanding, spreading through my body. I feel high on the sexual energy almost as much as the pot.

"I want more," I whisper, arching my back, pushing myself out for these boys.

"Yeah, baby," Noah whispers, tugging on my earlobe with his teeth.

At the same time, Beckett adds another finger, stretching me out, filling me up.

"And what about V, baby, can he finger you too?" The words feel so dirty as he whispers them to me, but I nod, giving my approval to Vaughn, who's eager to join in. He drops down next to Beckett, adding a finger next to the two already there and matching Beck's rhythm.

Every inch of my skin is tingling, a fire coursing through my veins. The warmth in my lower belly is ready to explode, and I can barely contain the feeling.

"Come for us, baby," Noah demands, as if he knows I won't last another fucking minute.

I explode around them, crashing over the waves of my orgasm with a harsh breath. "Fuck," I growl. "Fuck."

A deep, sinister chuckle roars from Noah's chest. "Get on your knees, baby."

I go down willingly, my knees hitting the soft area rug. I feel small with the four of them towering above me, fully clothed in comparison to my nakedness.

"Open your mouth," Noah demands, and I do, letting myself sink into the euphoria of my post-orgasmic haze. I open my mouth for him to stick two of his fingers in, the two that were just getting me off. I suck the heady, sweet taste of myself from his fingers, my eyes flickering up to meet his. There's a wash of approval coating his features with a touch of lust.

"You believe me now?" he taunts. I think he loves to see me like this, on my knees for him. The power dynamic is completely in his favor, all of their favors really.

I nod my head, and he pulls his fingers from my mouth with a pop. "Use your words, Mik," he growls.

"Yes," I whisper softly. "I believe you."

A small smile flickers across his mouth, turning his lips up ever so slightly. "I need you to prove it now, baby girl. Can you do that for me?"

A chill runs down my spine at his words. *Prove it.* I shouldn't be surprised that he needs my obedience, my loyalty, in order for him to believe me. He needs to see me listen to him, to fucking obey his words, for him to know without a doubt that I belong to him.

A year ago, I don't think he'd question where my loyalties lie. But ever since that night, everything about us has been in turmoil. My head is in a fucked up place, keeping me on edge at all moments.

Everyone has an idea, a theory, something they believe in.

Except me.

I have no memories, no inklings. Only a shit ton of emptiness and a head full of confusion.

But the weed has made things clearer. Stripping back all the layers of doubt, calming all the noise and leaving me with what's right in front of me.

I look up again, meeting Noah's dark eyes. He looks precarious, sinister even. A dark curl falls over his forehead as he stares down at me expectantly.

I feel the rest of them around me, stroking themselves and waiting for the okay to take what they want. They are waiting for me to agree, give my consent to what's about to happen here.

I nod.

"Words, Mikaela," Noah orders.

"Yes," I whisper first, and then repeat myself more clearly. "Yes." Because I do want this. Regardless of the subtext beneath the action. I yearn to be touched by them. I want to touch them.

I want everything that comes along with being on my knees for these four boys.

Beckett. Vaughn. Pax. *Noah.*

Hell, I think I even want the subtext. I want to prove my loyalty to them, to transport myself back to a time when all of this heaviness wasn't fucking weighing on me.

Noah smiles, this time wider, the corners of his mouth reaching up farther. "Such a good girl," he whispers, palming the side of my cheek.

It's stupid that the praise warms something inside of me. It should feel demeaning, I think. But instead, I love it; I work for it, for Noah's approval.

He gestures to someone, Vaughn, I think, but I don't move my head or take my gaze off him. Vaughn hands over something, and it takes me a moment to recognize the piece of fabric as the tie he had been loosely wearing.

"I'm going to cover your eyes," Noah tells me, holding the tie for me to see. "I want you to take care of my brothers. Can you do that, baby girl?"

I nod my head, agreeing, and Noah ties the fabric over my eyes, shielding me from seeing anything else. It heightens the experience, having one sense taken away. Everything else is in overdrive, each hand on my body setting my skin alight. I can distinctly smell the weed wafting off of Beckett, the coffee and cedarwood scent of Noah.

"Open," Noah says, and I feel something hit the seam of my lips with a light nudge.

I part my lips, allowing someone's cock to enter. I take him in slowly, savoring the taste as he glides into my mouth. I use my hand to assist me, stroking him while I suck and lick and tease. Eventually it becomes too much, and I can feel him tense in my hand. I pick up the pace, letting him sink his cock into me, hitting the back of my throat. He comes with a growl, which I'm certain belongs to Vaughn, letting the ropes of his cum hit the back of my throat. I swallow eagerly.

I only have a brief moment to inhale a deep breath before someone else comes to my lips, nudging me open. Hands run over my body while I work, caressing their way down until they reach my core.

"Open," I hear Noah's voice whisper coolly, and I comply, spreading my legs for him.

I'm dripping, and his hum of approval confirms it for me. He drags a finger achingly slow through my folds, gathering up the wetness and bringing it to my clit. One circle and then he abandons my swollen nub, leaving me aching for any glide of friction.

I moan around whoever is currently in my mouth, begging for the feeling, for relief to the ache that's building inside of me again.

It's not long until he comes too, pushing to the back of my throat and shooting his load deep into me.

I pant when he pulls out, sucking in all the air I can get.

"Get up," Noah orders, and I'm slower to comply this time. Dragging my needy body up to stand, reaching out for someone to guide me. Noah leads me over to one of the couches, instructing me to get on all fours.

Someone, I think it's Pax, if my guessing skills are right, brings his cock to the seam of my lips, while I feel Noah press into me from behind.

The fullness of the two of them makes me moan. I can barely control myself, can barely focus on pleasing either of them with all of the simultaneous stimulation. Noah brings a finger to my clit, flicking it over my sensitive button.

I'm writhing beneath them, barely able to contain myself

when I feel more hands on me. Running over my spine, palming my tits, and pinching my nipples.

Stars flicker in the back of my head as I crash over the edge of my orgasm. I don't know who comes first, Pax or Noah, but I feel them leave me as my head finally clears, bringing me back into the present.

The blindfold is removed, light hitting my eyes again, and instinctively, I close them at the sensation.

"How do you feel?" Noah asks, his hot breath hitting my cheek.

"Amazing," I answer.

Satisfied. Fulfilled. Worthy.

14

noah

Three Years Earlier

The first time I fucked Mik, I tried to be gentle. I barely knew her. We'd been dating for only a month, so even though I had the urge to snake my fingers around her neck or slap her ass, I restrained myself.

But the change from vanilla to kinky happened quickly.

My girlfriend is a spitfire, flipping her blonde hair over her shoulder and sinking to her knees for me with zero hesitation. She licks the length of my cock, circling her tongue over my balls before she finally puts me in her mouth. I groan at the feeling of my cock hitting the back of her throat. And when she looks up at me, there's water lining her big green eyes. She holds eye contact as she pulls back and releases me with a pop of her lips. I love the sight of her there, the lust lingering in her gaze while she sucks my cock.

It's not long before I'm hauling her up to her feet and pushing her onto my bed, dying to get a taste of her.

"Fuck me hard," she moans, and something unlatches in

my heart, as if it's expanding to love her more than I already do.

"How hard, baby girl?" I ask. A wicked smirk rises on her face.

Mik has hard edges, but underneath she's sweet. I've learned over the past month of being with her that she cries during movies, even when they're not that sad. She listens intently when people talk to her, and she's not the kind of friend that solves your problem. Normally after listening, she'll look you dead in the eye and say, "that sucks." She has a soft spot for animals and wants to pet every dog she sees. She donates to every cause she is told about, every chance she gets, even if only a dollar. She's a good person, a genuine one. In my life, that's a rarity.

"As hard as you can," she murmurs, a sexy edge to her voice.

The surface of my sweet girl is hardened, though. She has pain, deep cuts that money can't heal. She has a normal life, I think, happy family, and yet still she yearns for a release, something to take the edge off.

I slap her ass, a crack echoing through the room. She winces, a moment of pain etched on her pretty face, but then she smiles at me.

"You can do better than that," she taunts.

Heat floods my body at hearing those words. The permission I need to fuck her the way I want.

The roughness, the action of it all, is a release for both of us.

Something for me to get out of my head and a little pain for her to channel all her demons into.

I lean in, gripping her chin in my fingers while I continue to pump into her at the new angle. "Yeah, baby?" I coo. "Is this what you want? You want it to fucking hurt?" I squeeze her jaw while I taunt her.

"Yes," she mutters through gritted teeth. "Fuck me, Noah."

I do, slamming into her at a harsh pace. I nip at her lip, enough to draw blood and coat my mouth with the coppery taste. My hand drifts to her throat, gripping around the delicate skin. I can feel her pussy clench around my cock at the action. She's turned on, letting herself drift on the line between pleasure and pain.

She's moaning beneath me and squeezing my cock perfectly with her pussy. I can see it in her eyes, how fucking close she is to breaking, letting herself tumble over the edge and shatter beneath me.

I pump into her, the friction of our bodies so close together, stimulating her clit as I continue. When she finally comes, her eyes roll back, and she screams my name on repeat.

"Fuck, baby," I moan as she slowly begins to reopen her eyes. I love the look on her face when she tumbles off the edge, crumbling beneath me as her orgasm crashes over her.

So fucking beautiful.

Present

An exhausted and deeply satisfied Mikaela sleeps in my bed. There's a wash of pride that floods over my body seeing her there.

My girl.

Her eyes flutter as I wrap the soft blanket around her, tucking her in. "Where are you going?" she asks hazily when I don't lie down with her.

"Shh," I whisper. "Just back downstairs to see the boys out. I'll be back."

She hums an incoherent sound and turns, wrapping the blanket tighter around herself and drifting back to sleep.

I head back downstairs, finding the boys in different stages of post-nut. Beckett is leaning back into the couch, eyes closed and arms slung along the top with his shirt missing. Vaughn is back on the chair, fully clothed, but looking ready to pass out. Pax is also missing his shirt, his inked torso and arms on display while he stands in the center of the room, running a hand through his black hair. He looks more peaceful though, a rarity for Pax.

Their eyes float to me when I hit the bottom of the stairs. "Passed out?" Beckett asks, talking about Mik.

She's been stuck in her head, reliving memories since the minute she got here. She needs to take a break from the chaos. Her mind can be a hellish space. She needed to breathe again.

Other than the occasional cigarette, I've always tried to stay clear of drugs, but Mik has been drawn to weed since I met her. It's a love Beckett and her have shared, both of them trying to soothe their demons.

"Yeah," I tell him, "Knocked out." Mik's sex euphoria normally puts her right to sleep. I, on the other hand, get energized. On another night, I'd end up in my office, getting shit done, but tonight I'm aching to get back upstairs and feel her warm body next to mine.

It's been so long since she's let down her walls, let me in. I want to take advantage of every moment of it, in case she decides to build them back up again.

I take a seat on the loveseat across from Beckett. Pax finally stalls his pacing, instead moving to sit on the edge of the couch where Beckett is. All eyes are on Beck, waiting to hear how his conversation with Mik went.

Of the three of them, Mik has always been most likely to open up to Beckett. Maybe it's the lull of the weed or his pretty smile, but either way, it worked.

He sits up straighter, taking a breath for sharing. "She still doesn't remember."

Even though it isn't news to me, relief still sparks in my chest. It's been a whole year and Mik has barely even attempted to remember that night, to relive everything that happened. Even with all the pressure, with everyone begging her to say something, know something, she doesn't try.

She goes to therapy, but I don't think that has pulled anything out. No hypnotists. No doctors. Nothing else to try and recover from what she's missing.

I'm relieved, though. I'd rather keep those memories gone forever.

"What else?" I ask.

Beckett breathes in deeply, only to puff it out quickly. "She asked what I knew. I told her nothing. And she asked if I thought you did it." He chuckles softly. "I told her you didn't."

I stand up, walking over to clap him on the shoulder. "It worked," I tell him. "You did it."

Beckett smiles and turns his eyes down, avoiding meeting my gaze. "She's still fucked up, ya know."

I know. I know better than anyone else what that night did to her. It took the woman I planned to marry and turned her into a shell of herself. Just a broken girl trying to figure out how to live post trauma.

Mikaela was never the type of girl who had her entire life planned out. She was barely trying to make it the next minute. She wore demons on her sleeves, even though she had the type of life that should have made her happy.

Her demons matched mine in that way.

Rich kids aren't supposed to have problems, aren't supposed to be flawed, but that's what I was. Just a pretty boy harboring some fucking issues.

"I know," I tell him, running a hand over my jawline and sighing heavily. I still have shit to work through with Mikaela, and some of it we'll probably never work out, but step one was getting her to trust me again.

"What do you think is gonna happen when she remembers?" Vaughn speaks this time, asking the question that's probably on everyone's minds.

"It will ruin her," Beckett whispers.

People think they want the truth, like it's a fundamental right they deserve. But I think some things are better left hidden. Some truths will bury you, not bring you peace.

"If she hasn't figured it out by now, I don't think she ever will," I answer, voicing my hopes out as if it's reality. Sometimes that's how truth works. If you're confident enough, you can will anything into being true. You just need enough people to believe you.

"And your dad?" Pax asks this time, a single eyebrow lifting with the question.

My father is a whole other problem. We weren't on good terms before the incident, but this has fucked our relationship even further. I don't know if he ever plans on handing the company over to me, or if he just plans on holding it over my head for as long as possible. Something to dangle in front of me to keep me compliant.

I run a hand through my hair, messing it up more than it already is. "I don't know," I breathe. The guys nod their heads, staying quiet. I'm the key to our plan, to our end game. We each take what we want from our fathers and then the four of us will run this town. But first, we have to get them out of the picture. Something easier said than done.

Beckett stands, clasping a hand on my shoulder. "She'll come back to you, man." He voices lowly. "She's in there still."

I hang on to that. Hoping that he's right, that the love of my life is still in there somewhere.

That all of this will still wash away, and we'll be able to find ourselves again.

The truth can fuck off.

15

mik

Halloween - One Year Earlier

My parents don't answer when I call them for the third time. A flicker of shame washes over me when I realize that we announced the engagement to this entire party before I even told my parents. Noah doesn't quite understand, and this wasn't a surprise for him, so the people he wanted to be here are here celebrating with us.

My parents have claimed I've been distant since I met Noah two years ago. Well, my mother doesn't say a bad thing about Noah, so mostly it's been my father. I feel like this will be another nail in the 'I hate Noah' coffin.

"Come on." Noah gestures for me to get up and head back out to the party with him. I've spent the last twenty minutes holed up in his childhood bedroom, trying to get in touch with my family.

I hold the phone tightly in my hand, weighing my options. Wait here or wait downstairs. Either way, I had to wait for my parents to respond to me.

"Fuck it." I chug the rest of my champagne and slam the glass down onto the end table. "Let's enjoy our night."

Noah grins, extending his hand for me. I toss my phone back onto the bed and rise.

They can hear the news later. Right now, I want to celebrate.

Present

For the first time, I don't dream of Auden. When I wake, my face looks brighter. Softer and more vibrant. It's weird that I've been living with Noah for a week and somehow, I look better than I did when I walked through that front door for the first time.

I should probably look pale. Depressed, broken, something other than glowing and vibrant. Traitorous, that's how I should feel, and yet I don't.

I want to skip back onto the bed and let him fuck me again. Is there something wrong with me that he can fall back into my good graces so quickly? So easily.

It's only been a week, but it feels like years have passed.

A year of progress has been made in our seclusion. Noah works during the day, and I take online lectures and finish homework. At night, we sit at the dinner table eating whatever his parents' chef brought over and avoid hard conversations. Then later, I let him hold me in his arms and I sleep in his bed.

All the barriers I had tried to establish crumbled to the ground the minute I pledged my loyalty to him.

I fluff my blonde hair, noticing it looks shinier. I'm not sure why. It seems wrong that being back with Noah would bring me some sort of comfort. But it feels right. I spare a glance at the rock that weighs down my ring finger, and even that feels right.

Noah steps out of the bathroom with only a towel wrapped around his waist. His toned abs and chest are on display. The tattoos that wrap down his shoulder and to his forearms are showing, the black ink mesmerizing.

"You're coming with me today," he says as he steps up behind me, running his hands down my forearms and settling on my waist. He leans in, pressing a kiss into the spot between my neck and shoulders. A shiver races down my spine at the sensation.

"For what?" I ask, my voice leaving my throat in a hoarse whisper.

His eyes meet mine in the mirror I had been staring at myself in. They rake down my body, taking in the silk sleep shorts and camisole I'm wearing, and then move back up to my face. He studies me for a moment, looking for any signs that I'm a liar.

Even with my promise that I trust him, he's still guarded around me, as if I'm lying. Which is fair, considering the heavy plastic around his ankle is due to a video my family made.

"I have a hearing," he tells me, still studying me, watching how the features on my face respond.

"Okay." His answer doesn't trigger anything in me. I'm not sure why he's acting weird. As if he's hiding something, or I'm missing it. "I'll get ready." I spin in his arms, leaving a chaste kiss on his cheek before heading to the shower.

My mind is normally chaotic. It's loud and messy, hard for me to follow a single thought, but as I step into the shower, I realize how quiet my head has been. How normal I feel.

I can *breathe*.

There was a weight pinning me down before I started to

trust Noah again. It felt like I had to choose sides, him or my family. And every time I think about it, in the center of this whole mess is Auden, my baby sister who never did a thing wrong in her life.

How did she manage to fall victim to this game?

Picking Noah felt like betraying her. So instead, I chose to be unhappy. To be alone, confused, and fucking miserable.

That weight floated away the moment I decided to step back and just trust Noah.

I pick out a short-sleeved deep purple dress that's cinched at the waist. It's pretty and swings somewhere between casual and business casual. I don't do much with my face or hair, other than lightly dabbing some products on and releasing my hair from the elastic band.

I feel cute but understated. I don't want to draw any more attention than needed. I want to play my part, look like a good fiancée and nothing more. I don't want rumors started about me, or my appearance dissected.

When the media first got ahold of the story, the video played on repeat in the news. I tried to keep it off, avoiding all the discussion, but eventually, the need to know took over and I found myself glued to the television. I even used actual cable television, live news on my TV rather than reading it on the screen of my phone.

I needed to know. I was glued to the thing, waiting to hear something, someone else's account, anything to fill in the missing gaps.

But nothing came. It was all speculation. Criticisms ran rampant, mostly about Noah and the Bancroft family. All of the anti-rich came out in hordes to talk about how corrupted the Bancroft family is. His legacy was picked apart.

Even that held my attention. I knew a lot about the

Bancrofts, but professional researchers were able to dig up more dirt, and I hung on their every word.

It wasn't until they started in on my family that I had to turn it off and stop listening. Seeing my face on the screen was more than I could bear. There were journalists who wondered where I was when my sister came to the house to see me. What was I doing? Then inevitably, someone would share that I was too drunk, that I didn't remember. The look on the journalist's face would be priceless.

My sister was dead, and I was too drunk to remember even seeing her.

Shame coated my body. Every damn time.

I wasn't there for her the moment she needed me the most, and now every stranger in the world got to judge me for it.

I shake the thoughts from my head, forbidding myself from traveling down that train of thought again.

Instead, I slip the engagement ring back onto my finger, pair it with some sparkly earrings, and meet Noah downstairs.

He drives us silently in the Mercedes, and I don't ask for more details about what's ahead. Instead, I sink into the leather seat and listen to the music. I know he needs me to trust him, and subsequently, he has to trust me. He has a plan, something spinning in that head of his, and I realize I'm integral to it.

Beckett's words from the other night replay in my mind, *trial by media*. What happens in the courtroom means nothing if Noah can't win back the public, and I'm his key to doing that.

I'm not thrilled about it, but I don't think anyone expects me to princess wave as I walk beside him. My presence alone is enough to show my support.

Noah navigates the Mercedes into the pay to park lot

across from the courthouse. He said he had a hearing, but I'm not familiar enough with how criminal cases work to know what sort of hearings he should be having.

We walk across the street hand in hand to the courthouse. There are reporters lining the steps, cameras resting on shoulders and microphones ready to be shoved in our faces.

"No statement," Noah tells me, leaning in and whispering the words into my ears.

I didn't need to be told twice. I have no intention of talking to the people who stalk our every move and analyze us on live TV for entertainment. Noah wraps an arm around me, pulling me close as we walk through the hordes of reporters.

Inside the courthouse, we move through the metal detector, removing shoes and sending our personal items through the scanner before being allowed to enter.

David is already there when we get through security, a tan briefcase hanging from his fingertips while he stares at the watch on his opposite wrist. "Ready?" he asks when we approach. His eyes rake over me in a way that makes me uneasy. He's always assessing me, checking to make sure I fit the brand or that I won't freak out.

I think I'm the loose piece in this puzzle and he knows it. One wrong move and I could blow up this entire trial. I don't know if I actually have that much power, though. If I blew up this trial, I don't know what would happen, but I'm sure the Bancrofts wouldn't take it lightly.

"Are you ready?" David asks, his eyes landing back on Noah, who adjusts his navy suit, straightening the silver tie.

"Ready as I'll ever be," he says, a soft smile etched on his face. He's cocky, a normal attitude for him.

"What about her?" David nudges his face in my direction.

A sigh escapes Noah, his hand coming to the back of his neck nervously. "She doesn't know." Instantly, my body runs cold at his words.

"What don't I know?" I try to whisper the question so as to not draw attention to us, but anxiety is coursing through me now. I know he has secrets, I'm not naive, but I thought we were doing better. I thought he was being open with me.

Not waiting until we walk into a courtroom to tell me something, that judging by the look on David's face, is important.

"What?" I press when no one tells me.

A breath rushes from Noah's lips. "David's about to get this entire case thrown out."

That chill comes back to me. How? How deep do the Bancroft pockets run that they can get a criminal case thrown out?

"How?" I ask, the word leaving my lips in a hushed tone.

David shrugs his shoulders as if this is something he does every day. "Dirt," he replies simply.

"We got something on the DA," Noah elaborates. "They're going to drop the charges. This is just the official process."

"Why didn't you tell me?" I blurt out, this time slightly less discreet.

Noah pulls me into his side, pressing a kiss to the top of my head. "Shh, baby girl," he whispers.

"We can't do this here," David states, his eyes scanning the crowded hallway of the courthouse, making sure no one heard us.

"Trust me?" Noah asks in a whisper, that same phrase that he's been tying me to. He leans on it anytime my faith waivers, asking me over and over again, like one time I'll finally admit that I don't.

I'm trying to, damn I really am.

I swallow my pride.

"Yeah," I answer. "I trust you."

My parents aren't in the courtroom, and I take that as a small miracle.

Not many people are, really. Just the lawyers and us, not even a reporter is in here. The DA is a tall, well-dressed man. He looks clean and professional, shaking hands with David and Noah before they take their separate seats. I wonder what they have on that man to make him flush this case down the drain.

It has to be good, right?

My parents put a lot of trust in him. My mother would tell me while she unpacked groceries in my dorm room and I laid still under my covers, too fucking depressed to pull myself out. Every meeting they had with him, she would share the details.

They believed in him. They were sure he was going to be the one to finally solve Auden's case and punish her murderer.

I guess that makes them fools.

They never believed in the power of money and that's where they went wrong, I think. My father would have been content to be a starving artist for the rest of his life if it wasn't for having children. He only took the job with the Bancrofts in the first place to provide a better life for us.

The bailiff asks for everyone in the room to rise and the judge comes in as we do. He's an older man, a patch of graying hair on his head. He settles into the high seat at the front of the room, sliding his thick-rimmed glasses onto his face and shuffling through the papers on his desk.

"Mr. Miller." He finally speaks, addressing the DA. "You called this emergency hearing?"

"Yes, your honor. I would like to formally drop the

charges of murder in the first degree against the plaintiff, Noah Bancroft."

The judge huffs an indistinguishable response. "On what grounds?" he asks.

The DA coughs nervously, a crack in his polished exterior. "New evidence was brought to light."

"And what would that be?" the judge asks, his gaze trained on the DA.

I'm on the edge of my seat, waiting to see what he says. Waiting for the reasoning behind this dismissal.

The DA turns his head quickly, his eyes landing on me before turning back just as fast.

"The victim's sister came forward. She corroborated the plaintiff's story that the victim jumped that night. With this new evidence, we are no longer interested in pressing charges against Mr. Bancroft."

Ice shoots through my heart.

That's a fucking lie.

16

noah

Three Years Earlier

Judah answers the door when I arrive at the Wilder's house. He's not a fan of me and he doesn't keep it a secret. I'm not sure if he doesn't think I'm good enough for his daughter, or if he hates me because I have money.

It's like that sometimes. People hate you for something they want so desperately. My family's money is a blessing and a curse.

"Where is she?" I ask, and Judah sighs heavily. I can tell immediately he didn't want to call me. He never does.

But they don't know what to do when she gets like this, they don't know what to say or what to give her.

"Bedroom," Judah says, opening the door wider to let me in.

I give him a nod and move past him. I can't judge him for not knowing how to help his daughter. Mental health has a stigma around it, and as men, we're taught to shove our feelings down. So Judah Wilder doesn't know what to do about tears.

And then there's his wife, Sarah, equally uneducated. Not that I'm much better, but trial and error has taught me what Mik needs.

She's not crazy, contrary to the words whispered about her. Her mind is just a rough place to be sometimes. The drugs and alcohol surely don't help, and she's bad about taking the pills that keep her level. Sometimes it builds up and then she breaks down.

When I enter her room, she's on the floor at the foot of her bed, her arms wrapped around her knees while she sobs.

"I don't know what's wrong with me," she whispers between a sob, and I shake my head.

"Nothing's wrong with you, baby." I set the grocery bag I brought with me on the counter, fishing out the Xanax Beck got for me and the bottle of orange juice. "Open," I say, and she does, letting me place the white tab on her tongue. I hand her the juice and she swallows the pill down with a gulp.

I bend down, lifting her small frame up and bringing her to the bed, wrapping her in a fleece blanket and curling in behind her.

Her tears slow as she lets me hold her.

Sometimes she has bad days, filled with darkness, and everything seems like the end of the world. Other times, she's bright and fiery, full of life and love.

She experiences things differently than me in a way I can't quite understand.

I hold her tightly against my chest, staying quiet in case she wants to talk.

"I love you," she whispers softly before drifting off to sleep.

"I love you, too," I whisper back.

Present

The gavel pounds, and the shitshow is finally over.

I inhale a breath of air, and it feels fresher, fucking better, knowing that prison is out of the question. There's a glassiness hanging in Mik's eyes when I spin to face her. She looks sad, but she stands tall, holding herself together the best she can.

This will all pass. I hang onto that, knowing that soon this will all be over. A few more steps and we can lay this terrible mess to rest.

"You okay?" I ask.

She sucks in a breath and nods her head. "I'm fine," she says.

She's not fine, but I don't expect her to be.

"You need to give a statement," David drawls as he taps away on his iPhone, probably informing someone, likely my father, of the news. "And so does she," he adds, his eyes lifting from the phone to face Mik.

"She's not prepped," one of his assistants says from behind him.

"Then prep her," he snaps.

"I'm fine," Mikaela says, slicing a hand through the air to silence us. "I can give a statement."

"You sure?" David asks, an air of skepticism ringing in his voice.

"Yes." Her eyes meet mine. "Trust me?" she asks, using my own words against me.

I do trust her. I've always trusted Mik.

She loves hard, all-consuming. Which is why she's struggled so much since Auden's death. She can't handle the thought of losing someone she loves.

But that same logic applies to me, and that's why I trust her. Because I know she loves me, even though it's harder now, even if we struggle. At the end of the day, I know she loves me and keeping me here is worth more than her fear or pride.

"Always." I smile, and she matches the grin.

"I'm ready," she says, this time back to David.

David looks unsure; he doesn't know Mik the way I do. "Fine," he mutters. "But for the love of God, don't take questions."

A soft laugh escapes Mik's pink lips. "I can do that."

I'm relieved of my ankle monitor before we leave the room, air hitting the skin of my lower leg and reminding me once again that I've just won my freedom back.

I know what people are going to say. They're going to call this shady, that a sweetheart deal was made, but we can deal with the bad press. We'll make donations, build a school in Auden's honor, whatever it takes to secure my damn freedom.

As I feel the cool air hit my skin and let the leg of my slacks back down, I feel a rush of adrenaline. That thing has lived on my leg for over three months now, so having it gone is better than a breath of fresh air.

We head back out to the front steps of the courthouse where reporters wait, buzzing with the news. The hearing was called this morning, an emergency, giving no one notice and no opportunities to block it. The reporters are finding out about the hearing at the same time they're learning of the news that I'm a free man.

"Keep it short," David reminds me.

I do. Stepping in front of the press with Mikaela tucked into my side, I give them a short blurb. A quick few words about how thankful I am for this to be behind us and how I'm ready to grieve the loss of my future sister-in-law in private.

They look to Mik next, ready for her to say something.

"This has been a great tragedy for my family," she starts, a cold flicker rising in my heart, nervous about what she'll say. "I lost my younger sister almost a year ago now, and it devastated me and my family. Even worse was knowing that my fiancé was suffering as well. I don't blame my parents for their allegations. We all wanted someone to blame for this terrible thing, for what happened to my sister. But I can't in good conscience say an innocent man should go down alongside her. I've already lost one person I love, and I am very grateful that the legal system did its job and didn't take another loved one away from me." She pauses for a moment, looking at me with glassy eyes. "I'm still mourning the loss of my sister, and now, with this behind us, I'm ready to move forward." She gives the reporters a slight nod. "Thank you for your time," she says, full of fucking grace.

They hang on her every word, and when she finishes, they're raising their hands, their microphones, questions are being shouting.

"No other comments," Mik tells one, a soft smile on her face. She's so fucking nice, and they love it.

I wrap my arm around her waist tightly, dragging her into my side as we head back to the Mercedes. I can't wait to take her home, to show her how much I appreciate her right now.

I open her car door first, letting her get settled while I head around and get into the driver's seat.

"Just tell me one thing," Mik asks, her voice still sugary sweet. "Did you do it? Did you kill my sister?" That question cuts like a knife.

17

mik

Halloween Night - One Year Earlier

I'm already buzzed from the champagne I chugged. My mind is on the fast track, heading toward a euphoric daze. I immediately head down for more, more champagne, drugs—I'll take whatever I can get my hands on.

"There you are," Edward coos, and there's a lightness to him that's unusual. Noah's father is always stern and put together. I don't think I've ever seen him smile before tonight. But he smiles now, the corners of his lips rising steadily as he approaches me. "We've been wondering where the couple of the hour wandered off to."

He says we, but Mariam is nowhere in sight. "I was trying to call my parents," I say, a soft smile plastered on my lips as I try to sidestep him and make my way toward the bar.

"Let me get you something to drink," he says, as if reading my mind.

"Noah!" Beckett calls, stealing my fiancé's attention from me.

"Go," I tell him, shaking my hand out of his grip. "I'll get you a beer."

He leans in, kissing my cheek gently before heading off to find Beckett. I follow behind Edward toward the bar set up in the formal living room.

"Come with me," he says, gesturing for me to follow him to his office. "I have the good stuff tucked away in here."

I sit in front of his desk while Edward goes to the bar cart in the corner, grabbing a bottle of MaCallan.

"No, no." I shake my hand at him. "That's far too expensive, and my taste buds won't enjoy it. Save it for someone else."

Edward's taste in liquor surpasses mine by miles and the bottle he holds easily costs more than my car, my college education, and my parents' house combined.

"Nonsense." He chuckles, grabbing two low ball glasses from the cart and setting them on the island before us. "Taste buds be damned; you deserve a good drink." He pours a healthy dose into each glass. "Cheers."

We clink the two glasses together, and I bring mine to my lips, pouring the amber liquid down my throat. It burns its way down, and I can't control the wince that overtakes my features. "Shit," I groan.

Edward chuckles, taking my empty glass and setting it down on the cart. "You should sip it," he tells me, gesturing to his full glass.

"Next time," I tell him, standing and brushing my clammy hands against the smooth fabric of my dress. "I need something fruity after that." That elicits a chuckle from him.

I make a move to turn around and head back out to the bar when Edward grabs my arm, spinning me around in his grasp. "Mikaela." His dark eyes peer down into mine. "Are you happy?" he asks. "With my son?"

It's a weird question, I think. My dad asks the same thing all the time, as if he's waiting for the inevitable break-up. Am I happy? Of course I am. Anyone who sees Noah and I together could tell you that.

He's my anchor. The love of my life.

"Yeah," I say, disengaging my arm from his. "I'm very happy with Noah."

He smiles, not enough to show teeth, just the corners of his lips twitching upward. "Good," he tells me. "Welcome to the family, Mikaela."

Present

"Did you kill my sister?"

I've never actually asked him the question. To be honest, I wasn't sure I wanted to know. But now, after singing his praises, I did. I needed to know if I was a liar or not.

"It's already done," I add, watching the warmth leave his face, instead being replaced by a cold demeanor. A few minutes ago, he was on cloud nine, and I just fucking crushed him with one question.

But I needed to know.

"I won't change my statement. You're already free," I tell him. "I just want to know."

His eyes glance back out at the media, still on the courthouse steps on the other side of the street. If we weren't so close to them, I think he would reach out and grab me, but Noah is too composed to possibly risk causing another issue.

Instead, he grips his knuckles around the steering wheel, turning them white with the pressure.

"Seriously?" he asks. "What happened to trust?"

"It flew out the window when you tricked me."

He scoffs, a heavy breath rushing from his mouth. "And how exactly did I trick you?" he asks, venom dripping from the words.

"When you brought me here and fucking manipulated me," I scream, which causes Noah to give me a harsh look.

"Shut the fuck up," he growls. "We'll talk about this when we get home."

He shifts the Mercedes into gear quickly and pulls us out of the parking lot and onto the road with little effort.

His anger at my question only makes me more adamant. I've been compliant. I've trusted him like he asked. Now, in return, I want one answer.

"I've done everything you've asked since you dragged me to your house without even consulting me. The least you can do is answer one question." I lean back in the leather seat, my arms crossed over my chest.

"Yeah, Mik? And why should I?" he sneers, navigating the car onto the highway quickly. He's driving recklessly now, taking his anger out on the gas pedal.

I need to know without a doubt that he didn't do it. I need to know that I didn't just set my sister's murderer free.

Even if the answer kills me, I need to hear the truth.

Ever since that night, everyone has been trying to protect me, shield me. I don't want to be protected anymore; I want to know the truth. Even if it takes me down.

I try not to show that his driving scares me, not to reach for a handle. Instead, I press my ass into the seat and brace myself.

"She was my sister," I shout back.

His foot is still pressed down on the gas pedal as he sighs heavily, steering us onto the road.

"I didn't kill her," he finally says. He's still tense, teeth gritted.

I don't ask a follow-up question. I let him stew as he races us back to the house. I don't want to anger him any more than I already have, but I won't back down.

I deserve to fucking know after I just saved his ass.

He pulls into the driveway, slamming on the brakes until the car lurches to a stop. I'm thankful for the seatbelt that pushes me back into the leather after his quick stop.

Hastily, he exits the car, moving to my side to open the door and pull me out of the car by my dress, the fabric ripping as he does so. He drags me into the house, pulling me behind him even as I stumble in my high heels. Once inside, he swings the door shut and slams me into the foyer wall.

A hand snakes up to wrap around my throat. "Do you really think I would do that? That I *could* do that?" he asks, his pupils dark, nearly black as they look into my eyes.

"That you could kill someone?" I ask, the question coming out hoarse.

I do think Noah could kill someone. I wouldn't put it past him at all.

The Bancrofts aren't clean by any means. As one of the wealthiest families in the country, they've had their hands in many deaths. Been associated with scandals that would shock most people. But they always have a scapegoat, someone to take the fall and keep their name out of it.

"To you," he adds, a clarification. "Do you really think I could do that to you?"

No. The answer lingers on the tip of my tongue.

He's a bully. A prick. A colossal asshole.

But no.

I don't think he would hurt me like that. In other ways, sure, but not like *that*.

"No." I finally whisper the answer, the word hoarse from his hand on my throat.

Air comes easy as he drops his fingers from my neck. His arms shake, like he's trying to let go of something, and when his eyes drift back to mine, they're still dark but coated with sadness.

He shakes his head at me, and then turns away, leaving me panting for air in the entryway.

"Wait," I call after him.

"Leave it the fuck alone, Mik," he growls, waving a hand to dismiss me. He marches over to the liquor cabinet, pulling a pricey bottle of whiskey from the top shelf and popping it open. He brings the bottle to his lips, not even bothering with a glass as he takes a long chug.

My stomach burns at the thought of even drinking that. Bile threatens to rise up at the sight. Ever since that night, the sight of whiskey has made me nauseous.

"I'm sorry," I blurt out. "I was…" What was I? Scared? Ashamed? Embarrassed? All of the above. "I trust you, I do. I just don't know what to think." I throw my hands up. "It's all too much sometimes, ya know? And I constantly feel like I have to choose. You. My family. Auden." My voice cracks when her name leaves my lips. "Why can't I just love you all?" I feel the tears threatening to escape as I plead with him.

Finally, he spins on his heel, the bottle still firmly in his grasp. His dark eyes peer over me. My dress is ripped at the collar, the dark purple fabric hanging limp over my tits and exposing the top of my bra.

"You have to choose," he tells me, no trace of emotion in his words. "And you have to choose me, baby girl. I can't protect you if you don't." He brings the whiskey to his lips and takes another long gulp.

"Protect me from what?" I ask, the question coming out whiny. I'm exhausted from hearing the same spiel over and over again.

Trust me.

It's for your own good.

I need more than that. Reasons, evidence, anything to tell me why I'm trusting him.

"Take that off," he demands, using the bottle to gesture toward my dress. He completely ignores my question, instead switching tactics.

There's a heat in his eyes and his gaze is trained on me.

I obey, if only because his words light a fire in my core, and I hope that this action will get me one step closer to the truth.

Slowly, I pull up the fabric of the dress, lifting it over my head and dropping it next to me on the tiled floor. Noah's eyes are trained on me, watching every movement as I bare myself for him.

I wonder if it's the symbolic act for him, the idea that every time I peel off the layers of clothing, I'm opening myself up for him, with one less barrier he has to break through to get back to where we were.

It's strange how much can change in one night.

I fell asleep in love.

And I woke up broken.

For the past year, I've been fighting everyone. Him, my family, my fucking head. Nothing falls into place; nothing is right anymore.

I thought I wanted to be numb, that I wanted to be catatonic, to avoid all of the damage spiraling in my head. But now, I think I just want his hands on my body, his harsh words. I want him to fuck me until I can't remember anything at all, until it all just melts away.

His gaze lights a fire underneath my skin, burning its way through my body. Slowly, his legs stalk toward me. The soles of the Italian leather shoes hitting the ground are all I hear as he makes his way over. He abandons the half-filled bottle on the entryway table in favor of bringing his hands to me, running them down my bare shoulders.

"Fucking beautiful," he murmurs, his hands still on me, exploring every inch of my skin.

His lips hit mine next, and nothing about this kiss is soft or sweet.

It's harsh and demanding. He takes what he wants from me, what he needs. Holding me tightly with his hands gripped onto my hips. I let him take the lead, let him take control. It's what we both need right now.

He pushes me back against the front door, one hand pressed against my chest to hold me in place while the other runs down my body.

"I thought you trusted me, baby girl." His voice is so low, I almost miss the words that escape his lips.

He's still angry, pissed off at me for standing my ground, for demanding answers.

"I do," I tell him, my eyes focused on him. "I can trust you and still want answers at the same time, Noah."

A sting burns across the side of my thigh, and I realize he just slapped me. He runs his palm over the red flesh. "Mik," he growls. "Don't fucking test me right now."

"Why?" The burning inside of me has only made me more confident.

More willing to play his game.

His eye twitches, a quick movement that anyone else would have missed, but I'm so close to him, staring into his eyes, and I see it. It's the anger in him that he's trying so hard to hold back.

But I don't want him to.

I want him to let it all out.

We're in this together. All this anger, all this fucking pain, is ours to share.

"Say it," I urge him, and his grip on me tightens, his nails biting into my flesh. "Say what you're thinking!"

A snarl passes his lips, venom dripping from the sound. "Yeah, baby girl? You don't even know what you're asking for."

"I can handle it," I shoot back.

He chuckles, a sinister sound. "You can't handle shit, baby. You blocked out a whole fucking night to avoid the truth."

The words cut into me, deep lacerations into my soul.

But I asked for that. I asked for him to tell me, to hurt me.

"That's not fair."

Another malevolent chuckle leaves his lips while he spins around, this time pressing the front of my body against the door. He grips a fistful of my hair, turning my head so my cheek hits the wood door while he holds me in place.

"You don't know, baby. You have no idea what's fair in this world because I protect you from everything. And that's fine by me. I would die for you, Mikaela. But you don't fucking get it." His fist tightens with the statement, pulling my scalp back farther.

I groan in protest from the bite of pain on my scalp.

"All I ask is for you to trust me, baby girl, and you can't even do that." His words are filled with pain.

"I do trust you," I say, but the words come out in a harsh whisper.

I hear the crack of his palm hitting my ass, and the pain reverberates through me. I yelp out, but he does it again and again until I'm nearly crying. My lashes are coated with wetness, and I hear my voice, a small sound begging him to stop.

"You're a liar," he tells me, the words laced with venom.

He peels the lacy pair of panties I'm wearing down my legs, guiding me to step out of them. Nudging my ankles with his heel, he instructs me to widen my stance.

I'm whimpering, practically begging for him to touch me, to fuck me.

He doesn't disappoint, freeing his cock from the black slacks he's wearing and hoisting me up so I can wrap my legs around him. He drives into me at a brutal pace, taking everything I have to offer.

I'm soaked, every inch of me ready to be used by him.

My eyes squeeze shut as the sensations begin to wash over me while the throbbing flesh of my ass hits the doorframe over and over again.

"Look at me, baby girl." His deep tenor pulls me out of my head and back to the surface. "I want you to look at me while I fuck you."

My eyes shoot open, locked onto his dark ones.

He doesn't let up his rhythm. The only time he slows is to adjust his grip as he brings a hand down to my pussy, running his thumb over my clit.

My eyes shut as my orgasm wrecks me, stars shooting in the back of my eyelids. I scream out his name, I'm not sure how many times.

I'm panting when he follows me over the edge, losing himself inside me. Then slowly, he lets me down, my legs too weak to stand, so I sink to the floor in a puddle of myself.

The taste of his name still lingering on my lips.

18

mik

We're in limbo, Noah and I, somewhere in a state between trust and distrust. Neutral.

I don't leave his house. I spent the night after he fucked me against the front door. I even slept in his bed with his arm wrapped around me, the ring he gave me still on my finger.

But we don't talk. We spend the time with the silence stretching between us.

What's left to say?

"I believe you," I blurt out.

Noah's spoon hits the glass bowl of cereal he's eating. He looks up to meet my eyes, his mouth still filled with a bite of Cocoa Puffs. My own cereal has turned to mush in its milky broth, staining the milk brown with the chocolate flavor and making everything wet and soggy. I push the bowl away from me.

"I believe you," I repeat when he doesn't respond. The words have been on the tip of my tongue since he walked away from me last night.

He swallows the bite of cereal in his mouth and brings

the napkin to his lips, wiping himself off and folding it neatly before he responds. "What changed?"

"Nothing," I answer quickly. "I asked you a question, and you answered. I believe you."

He nods his head and mulls over my statement. His dark hair is unruly. He needs a trim to keep the messy curls from dropping onto his forehead. As if he notices me scrutinizing his hair, he sweeps a hand through it, pressing it all back. "I wish you never doubted me," he says.

I suck my bottom lip in between my teeth. It's not that I ever doubted him, per se. "I just... I don't know what to think anymore. It's a lot."

He nods his head, bringing another bite of cereal to his lips. "I get that," he says between bites. "But you need to tell me stuff like that. Trust me, hmm?"

I open my mouth to respond, to repeat that I do trust him, but the ringing of my phone interrupts me.

"Hello," I answer.

"Mikaela." My mother's voice rushes through the speaker. Suddenly the events of yesterday come crashing back to me.

The charges were dropped.

I made a public statement defending Noah. Something that directly conflicts with their story.

"Mom, I'm so sorry." The words leave my lips hastily.

"It's not that." She cuts my apology short. "I need to show you something. Can you meet me?"

My eyes glance up at Noah. He's been controlling lately. Dragging me here and not letting me leave. But he can't control me, and I'm allowed to see my family. I'm a grown adult.

"Yeah," I tell her. "Where?"

"The coffee shop that..." She trails off, choking on her words. "The one that Auden liked."

It's funny how a simple sentence, a location, can elicit so many memories. Coffee dates with my sister come flooding back to me. We loved that damn café. They made pumpkin spice lattes in the fall and had high wooden shelves lined with books. Auden and I could spend hours there on a Saturday. Me with a book in my hands and Auden with her homework. Both of us sipping lattes and people watching.

I think I liked her the most in that coffee shop, in some weird way. Those moments with her were fun. That's how I remember my sister, curled up in a leather wingback chair, ankles crossed beneath her, and her pin-straight auburn hair falling in her face.

"Yeah," I tell her. "I'll be there soon."

Noah is looking at me expectantly when I hang up the phone, dark eyes wide and focused on me. I can't just up and leave because I don't know where my car is, probably still parked on campus.

"Can you take me to get my car?" I ask, letting the words slip from my lips in a sugary sweet tone.

His eyes narrow suspiciously. "For what?"

"My mom wants to see me, and I also just want my car back."

He stares at me for a few moments, probably trying to figure out how to say no. "I'll come with you to see your mom," he finally says.

"No," I counter quickly. "It's too soon." Considering my mother still thinks Noah killed her daughter, the last thing he should be doing with his newfound freedom is flaunting it in front of her.

A heavy sigh leaves his lips. "I'll sit outside." He brings another spoonful of cereal to his mouth, his silent way of ending the conversation.

"I'm a big girl, Noah. I can go on my own."

He studies me again, as if he's waiting for me to back

down under the weight of his gaze. His cold eyes bore into me, silently questioning me.

What does he think is going to go wrong?

Noah's always been protective, demanding, and just fucking controlling. But this is a whole new level; his need to be a part of every second of my life. I can't understand, can't grasp his reasoning.

I'm not in danger.

"Fine," he finally says, pushing the empty bowl away from him. "I'll take you to get your car, and then you can go see your mom. One hour, Mik," he says with a stern look. "Don't take any longer than that. "

"Aye aye, captain," I mock, using my hand to salute him. His dark eyes only grow more irritable with me.

But fuck that. I'm allowed to have a life outside of him.

MY MOM IS SETTLED at a small round table in the back of the café near the chairs Auden and I used to lounge in. Business is slow on a Tuesday morning. Just a few customers lined up at the coffee bar and a few scattered about at tables.

Her eyes are glassy when I reach her table, and she looks up at me with sadness.

"I'm sorry," I say again, a gut reaction to seeing her hurt.

She cried a lot after Auden's death. She was heartbroken, we all were, but she just showed it more. I don't think my dad cried a single tear, not that he wasn't mourning, he just had to show strength for us over a week of preparations, viewings, and the funeral. A tear never left his eyes, at least not while anyone could see.

She leaps from the chair and wraps her arms around me. "It's okay," she whispers. "I'm not mad."

I lean into her hug, finding comfort in her warm embrace and soft words. "I just..." I trail off. "I believe him," I whisper to her.

She pulls back, hands still gripped on my shoulders but giving herself a better view of me. "It's okay, Mikaela. It's okay if you believe him."

I feel my own eyes start to water, wetness lining the rim of my lashes.

"Here, sit," she says, gesturing for me to take a seat at the table with her. She settles in the seat across from me, her hands clasped in front of her on top of a manila envelope. She's nervous, twisting her fingers around and chewing on her bottom lip.

"Mom... What's going on?"

She fingers a piece of her blonde hair, twisting it around while she avoids eye contact with me. "The DA brought us something they found during the investigation."

"Okay, so?" I prod.

Slowly, she opens the envelope, pulling out a few sheets of white paper. She slides them across the café table until they're in front of me.

"What is this?" I ask, lifting the papers to read them closely.

It looked like messages from my number and then... from Auden's.

Auden, 11:00 PM: Mikky, I need you.

Auden, 11:01 PM: Please answer.

Auden, 11:05 PM: I need you to come pick me up.

Auden, 11:06 PM: PLEASE

Auden, 11:07 PM: Where are you?

Auden, 11:08 PM: ???

Auden, 11:12 PM: I'm scared.

My chest caves, sinking into my chest so quickly it hurts. Instinctively, I grab at it, trying to hold my heart, protect it from all of the pain currently wrecking it. I can't control the tears that spill over my lashes, dripping down onto the paper in large droplets.

This can't be real.

"What is this?" I ask my mother, heaving a breath.

"Mik," she coos, reaching across the table for my hands and holding them within her own. "Mik, they're text messages from that night. Auden sent them to you."

I can't breathe, my lungs burn, fire racing through them. She had been trying to text me, trying to call me that night. Less than an hour before she died.

Where was I?

I squeeze my eyes shut, willing anything to come back to me at that moment. What was I doing when my sister was begging me for help? I can't even remember where I left my phone, if I was even holding it when she was texting me.

"I never saw these," I tell her frantically.

"I know." She squeezes my hands.

A thought comes to mind, and I pull my phone from my bag. I never delete messages, and since she died, I specifically never deleted Auden's. I pull up the messages app, searching for her name.

I spin the phone to show my mom.

Auden, 9:00 PM: Thank you for the pep talk. Say hi to Noah!

Mikaela, 9:00 PM: Love ya. Stay safe! Wink, wink.

"I don't have those on my phone. Mom, I haven't deleted a single message from her. Why would I delete those?"

She studies the phone, reading the last messages I exchanged with my little sister. *Wink, wink.* I cringe. I had forgotten she planned to have sex for the first time that night.

I clench my hand over my stomach, suddenly feeling like

I might throw up. Was that why she was coming to me? Did something happen with the boy she was interested in?

"Mikaela?" My mom's voice breaks through the noise in my head. "It's okay," she coos.

"It's not." I try to keep myself from yelling, but it's hard with the ringing in my head and the tears that are free falling now. "She needed me! She was calling for help and I wasn't there. I should have been there to help her."

She leaves her seat, coming around the table to hold me, rock me in her arms like I'm a baby again. "I know, sweetheart, I know."

19

mik

Halloween Night - One Year Earlier

I leave Edward in the kitchen, making my way out to the bar to get a drink that doesn't burn my throat. The bartender hands me a glass of champagne that I drink happily, and a bottle of beer for Noah.

I wander through the party, the heels of my black boots clicking against the tiled floors as I search for Noah.

I'm not surprised to find him out back, reclined in a wide-legged stance on one of the patio chairs. Beckett is next to him, bringing a joint to his lips and puffing out a cloud of smoke.

The alcohol has made my head lighter, happier, so I find myself skipping over to them. Noah smiles as I approach, reaching out for a hit of Beckett's joint.

"Nah." Beckett pulls it away, instead digging in his pocket. He pulls out a small, sealed baggie with a few pieces of candy inside. "Edibles." He laughs, pulling one out and handing it over to me. "Try it."

It looks like a tiny square sour gummy. "How high will this get me?"

"Dude." Beckett smiles. "These things will fuck you up. But you're about to be a married woman, right? You need to party before this one chains you down." He chuckles, reaching over to nudge Noah.

I pop the candy in my mouth. It's flavored like weed covered in sugar. "Ugh." I take a chug of my champagne. "Beck, that doesn't even taste good!"

He shrugs a shoulder. "Why does the taste matter? It's supposed to get you high."

The champagne washes down the flavor. Nothing should taste like pot; it's not something you want to eat. Smoke, sure, but eat?

Noah only laughs, pulling me down to sit in his lap and wrapping his arms around me. Soft kisses meet the curve between my neck and shoulder, gently nipping. "You know something, Mik?" Noah whispers low, only loud enough for us to hear. "I really fucking love you."

I DON'T KNOW how to process the information my mother just handed me.

The knowledge that Auden was reaching out to me, searching for me, and I wasn't there for her grates on my nerves. Burns my soul to fucking ash. I should have been there for her. I should have known.

But I wasn't.

I don't even know what I was doing. What was more important than my sister?

It takes me a while to calm down in the coffee shop before I leave. Mom wants me to stay or to let her drive me, but I need to go. I need to be alone.

I drive the Beetle around for a while until I find myself pulling into the familiar cemetery. Her plot is in the middle of a sea of gravestones. Even in the late afternoon, with the October sun shining down on me, the graveyard feels ominous.

There're only endings here. Things that never happened. Dreams that will never come true.

Only one other person is in sight, kneeling in front of a stone with a bouquet of flowers in his hands.

I walk past him, toward my sister's grave.

In an effort to be different, my parents had her gravestone carved from granite in the shape of a soccer ball. The ornate thing cost $10,000 and came right out of Auden's college fund. Not that she'd ever be able to use it anyway.

It's funny, I think, how much money we waste on the dead.

There's a quote by Anne Frank that reads, *"Dead people receive more flowers than living because regret is stronger than gratitude."*

I think about that every time I come here and scan my eyes over the freshly planted flowers, the decor that's placed in front of each stone. So much work and effort go into taking care of something for someone who's not even here anymore.

Auden's stone has a cluster of figurines in front of it. An angel, a teddy bear, a soccer ball. The flowers my mom planted in the spring have died, but there're fresh flowers in a vase. It's silly how we leave all these things here for her.

When she died, her coffin was stuffed. Friends and family came with mementos, pictures, shirts, knickknacks. Anything that held significance was placed in the coffin and buried with her, as if she'd ever be able to use them again.

Regret, I think.

I have more regrets than I can count when it comes to

Auden. All the times I kicked her out of my room, told her to leave me alone. Every time I refused to let her borrow my clothes or my makeup. I would whine about having to drive her places, slamming the door and accusing my parents of loving her more.

I would do anything to rewrite those moments. To not yell or scream. To let her wear my damn clothes. Hell, I'd give her my entire makeup collection.

I'd do anything if it meant having my baby sister back.

I don't even realize I'm crying until the tears drip off my face. I find myself on my knees in front of the granite soccer ball, my tears turning me into a mess.

"I'm sorry," I whisper, even though I don't believe she can hear me.

I don't know if there's anything after this life or where she might be now. But on the off chance that she can hear me, I want her to know I'm sorry. If I could, I would do it all differently.

I want her to know that even through all my bickering and whining, I truly did love her.

BY THE TIME I get back to the house, Noah looks pissed off.

"You don't answer your phone?" he asks when I walk in. He's on me in a second, pressing me back against the door. Dark eyes meet mine, peering down at me.

"I'm sorry," I mutter.

A knock sounds on the door, reverberating through the wood so I can feel it on my back.

"It's Beck," Beckett calls and Noah loosens his grip on me enough to step out of the way and let Beckett in. His eyes roam over the two of us, assessing our current state. I'm sure he could hear Noah yell at me through the door.

I wonder what they think, all of the inner circle, when they see us like this.

The screaming. The yelling. The making up.

When we're good, we're really good. But when we're bad… we're fucking toxic.

"You're lucky I had Beck follow you," Noah snarls, slamming the door closed behind Beckett.

"Seriously?" I ask, both of my hands finding the curves of my hips, my eyes locked on him. "You needed to have me followed?"

He tosses me a glare, a silent gesture warning me to shut up.

Another day, I might have. But right now, there's a fire coursing through my veins. The news of Auden's text messages is still fresh in my mind. My heart is already split open, and I have nothing to lose at this point.

"What about trust?" I ask, my hands reaching out in front of me and pushing against his chest.

It feels like everything comes to a standstill at the action. Noah doesn't flinch, not even moved an inch by my shove, but his eyes become darker, glaring at me as if the action was more damaging than it seems. Beckett sucks in a sharp breath, silently watching us.

"You're asking me that?" he asks, a slight laugh escaping his lips. "That's rich, Mik."

I cross my arms over my chest, attempting to stand my ground while also backing myself up against the wall. "Noah—"

"No," he cuts me off, jabbing a finger in my face. "I trust you, Mik. I do, deep down, I do. But you don't even know who you are lately. You're confused, and I don't trust that version of you."

His words cut through me, going straight for my heart

and adding themselves to the pile of hurt that Noah has caused.

"She texted me that night. Did you know that?" A flicker of something washes over Noah's features, but it's gone too quickly for me to understand what it was.

"Yeah? What'd she say?" he asks, stuffing his hands in the pockets of his jeans as he takes a step back from me.

"You know," I say, and this time it's me who steps forward, invading his space. "You're the one who deleted them, right? Hid all the evidence that my sister was trying to contact me? That something happened to her? You're always trying to protect me, right?" I ask mockingly. "So this was you?"

Air rushes from his lungs as he runs a hand through his thick black hair. "Mik—"

"So, it's a yes?" I cut him off.

He speaks of trust so damn often, constantly holding it over my head as a mold I need to fit, but he doesn't trust me. He just wants me to fit into his life, but he doesn't give a damn about how he fits into mine.

"Fuck you!" I growl. My hand lashes out, swiping over the entryway table and knocking all the contents to the ground. A vase shatters and car keys go flying. I see Beckett flinch out of the corner of my eye, but Noah doesn't. He closes his eyes, inhaling deeply, and then focusing on me again.

"You're overreacting," he says.

That only makes it worse, and this time I march away, looking for something else to wreck. When I enter the living room, the first thing I notice is Pax and Vaughn sitting on the couch. Fitting that they're here to witness my outburst.

I go to the credenza. There's a clay statue there he

bought at some art auction. I smash that first, letting the pieces shatter on the hardwood floors.

I fucking love the sound.

I don't stop. Anything within reach comes crashing down. Art, vases, everything.

Noah doesn't interrupt and neither do the boys. They let me tear everything down, break as much as I can.

No one speaks until I'm out of breath, on my knees, crying.

20

noah

I need to hit something. Channel this fucking anger I feel into something other than her. She's in tears in front of us, on her knees and panting as she comes down from her rage. All of us are staring at her after witnessing her complete breakdown.

That's what that was. After nearly a year of sucking in her emotions, storing them all away in neatly labeled boxes in the back of her mind, she broke. Your mind can only handle so much, can only pack away so many emotions before they start busting out at the seams.

And hers have exploded. A year of regrets bursting from her and taking her down with the wreckage.

"You did this," she cries out once her breathing has slowed down some.

"What are you talking about?" I grumble.

"You did this. You killed her," she shouts, the tears falling down her cheeks in waves now.

I feel my eyes glaze over with red, one of them twitching as a switch in my brain is pulled. Anger is creeping up through my veins, begging to explode out of me.

"Watch her," I grumble, hoping one of them will listen to me as I march away, heading for my home gym.

I need to clear my head or I'm going to do something I regret. I can't be near her right now, can't bear to hear the accusations that are about to leave her lips.

"Don't let her fucking leave," I yell, knowing one of the guys will hear me.

I don't even bother changing into workout clothes and head straight to the punching bag in the corner. The fitted jeans and white t-shirt will have to do for now. I slip my hands into the boxing gloves, not even bothering to ensure they're tight, instead launching right in. I slam my fists into the bag, feeling my knuckles clench beneath the material of the glove. I repeat the action over and over again, using every last ounce of energy I have to beat the shit out of the inanimate object.

I imagine my father, his smug grin staring right at me, waiting for me to fail. For this all to blow up in my face.

Hiding the truth from her was a commitment from the start, but one that is worth it. I have to remind myself repeatedly, this is the right thing to do.

I'm not sure how long I'm there, punching until all of the energy has drained from my body. I keep going even after my arms are sore and my body wants to stop. I keep punching the bag, trying to remove every last bit of anger from inside of me.

"Noah." It's Beckett's voice that breaks me out of the cage inside my head, halting my movements. My elbows hit my knees while I attempt to catch my breath. "She doesn't know." Becket continues. "She has no idea what you've done. She's just fucking confused." Beckett is silent for a moment, his bottom lip tucked between his teeth. "Maybe you should tell her," he says.

"No," I snap, righting myself. "She can't fucking know."

"Noah—"

"No," I repeat, cutting Beckett off. "She can't know. You think that was fucking bad?" I fling my arm, gesturing toward her breakdown in the living room. "Imagine if she knew the truth."

Beckett flinches at my tone. "I know, but I think not knowing is killing her."

He's not wrong, and I know that. The missing moments, the fragments of memories, are breaking Mik. She longs for answers to her missing memories, and I wish I could tell her.

But I can't.

"No," I say again. "She can't fucking know, Beck. Got it?"

Beckett holds up his hands defensively. "Got it," he repeats.

I go back to punching the bag even though my body feels weak, pounding my fists against the material, letting every sliver of energy out. Leaving it all here on this mat. A ringing interrupts me, taking Beckett's attention as well.

I rip the gloves from my hands and pluck the ringing phone from my pocket, bringing the device to my ears.

"What?" I growl.

"That's how you answer the phone for your father, hmm?" My dad's voice lectures through the speakers.

"Yeah," I grumble. "What do you need?"

"Your mother wants to have a party tomorrow night. She wants you and Mik to come to celebrate this whole ordeal being past us now."

Ordeal. Like this is just some hiccup that's passing by. Not that a girl is dead. Another is broken. And I'm left scrounging up my dignity and putting the pieces back together.

"A party?" I scoff. "You really think that's a smart idea?"

He grumbles on the other end of the line. "Yeah, Noah.

And it would make your mother happy, so you need to get your girl and yourself over here tomorrow night. Got me?"

"Yeah, whatever," I spit. "We'll be there." I jab the red button with my finger and stuff the device back into my pocket. I'm even more riled up now. The last thing I want to do is go to my parents' house, let alone bring Mik back there.

"Fuck." I smack my fist into the punching back, the knuckles cracking from the pressure.

Guess we're going to another fucking party.

21

mik

Halloween- One Year Earlier

Everything feels... different.

My body is heavy, each limb feels like it weighs a thousand pounds, and moving them is unbearable. I don't know what time it is, or what we're even doing. The living room couch in the Bancroft estate is made for viewing, making the thing incredibly uncomfortable, but I'm too heavy to shift my position, so instead I stay.

When I close my eyes, I fall deep into my subconscious. Everything here is cartoon-like. I think I'm watching an animated show of my life inside the walls of my mind. It's entrancing. I watch the figures move through my mind, unsure of what's propelling them or where they're going.

Suddenly they become angry, violent. They're lashing out at each other.

"Mik?" It's the sound of Noah's voice that brings me back to the present, back to the living room. My eyes open, taking in the sight of him. "You okay, baby?" he asks, his brows pinching in concern.

"Yeah," I reply, my voice hoarse, and my throat feels raw.

He nods, but the concern is still etched on his face. "Auden's here," he tells me, and I look behind him to see my baby sister.

She's glistening with sweat and tears have rolled down her eyes, smearing the glittery eye makeup she had applied earlier. She hiccups on a sob when I look at her and then rushes in to hug me.

"Mik," she cries my name.

I want to ask her what's wrong, but the words don't leave my lips.

The room becomes darker around me, and the cartoons come back, taking over everything in my line of sight.

Still angry, so fucking angry.

"Stop!" I shout, but they don't listen.

"Leave me alone!" I try to no avail.

They're chasing me, hunting me, and before I know what I'm doing, I run.

Present

It's Beckett who leaves first after Noah, leaving just Vaughn and Pax to hover over me with concern coating their features.

If I had any energy left, I would go after them too.

Punch, hit, kick.

Fucking scream at them. They did this too. They brought me here, made me relive this fucking hell over and over again, and the whole time they were lying.

Everything was a lie.

All a ploy to bring me here, to make me believe in Noah, and help his case.

I drop my face into my palms. I'm embarrassed, humiliated to be taken advantage of. I can't help but to think Auden would be so disappointed in me.

Vaughn only walks away to type into his phone furiously, but Pax stays in the destroyed living room with me, sitting on the edge of the chair with his eyes glued to me.

I'm not sure how long we sit like that until I hear someone enter the house. "What do you need?" A soft female voice interrupts my spiral. I hear Vaughn respond to her in a hushed tone before her heels click against the hardwood floor as she enters the living room. "Jesus," she mutters.

Her eyes drift over the destroyed room, over the shards of glass, the painting with a hole torn through the center. "What happened?" Her eyes drift from Vaughn to Pax to me. "Are you okay?" she asks, her voice gentle.

She rushes over to me, the nude pumps she's wearing clicking against the floors. Her legs are clad in dark denim, and she wears a white silk blouse underneath a trench coat. Sleek and effortless. Even her hair looks perfect, deep brown locks falling in loose waves.

"I don't know." The words come out broken, the sobs of a crying girl.

She wraps me in a hug before I even know what's happening. Enveloping me with her warm embrace. "It's okay," she whispers. "You're okay."

I feel myself relaxing in her grasp, her words easing my tension. "We're going to breathe," she tells me, and then she starts breathing deeply, her eyes sealed shut and her hands wrapped around mine.

I do it, if only because she's a friendly face amongst the chaos.

Inhale.

Exhale.

The air fills my lungs and eases the anxiety that's building inside of me. She's pretty, and the kindest face I've seen in a while. I'm not sure who she is to Vaughn, or why he called her here, but I am happy to have someone other than them.

Her green eyes meet mine once I'm calm and the tears have stopped flowing. "Now," she says, a small smile rising on her cheeks. "I'm going to yell at these boys, and I don't want you to worry about it." She smirks and rises to her feet. "What the fuck did you do to her?" she asks sternly and loudly, the tone forcing Vaughn to take a step back.

"Nothing." Pax growls. "She did it to herself."

"Yeah?" The girl jabs a finger at him. "She got that worked up all by herself, hmm?"

"Laurel," Vaughn hisses. "I told you not to ask fucking questions."

She steps up to Vaughn next, inches from his face. "You can't ask me to come over here and not ask questions." It's an amusing sight to see, since she's a whole half foot shorter, trying to go head-to-head with him. Vaughn looks like he barely knows what to do with a woman who isn't meek.

"She's fine," Vaughn shoots back at her. "You are just here to comfort her." His tone is harsh.

"She needs to pull it together," Noah says, entering the room. "Because my parents are having a celebration tomorrow night and she needs to be there."

This has me moving, rising to my feet and matching Laurel's anger. "You don't think I've done enough?" I shout at Noah. "This charade is over."

Noah gets to me in seconds, leaping over the couch and grabbing me by the chin, forcing me to look at him. "Nah, baby girl, you don't get to say when this is over. You still have an act to play."

I yank myself from his grasp, rubbing a hand over my chin. "Fuck you, Noah," I sneer.

A smirk rises across his lips, and he backs me up farther until he's pressing me against the wall with his hard body. "Been there, done that. And I'll be doing it again." He laughs coolly. "Suck it up, baby girl. You're going tomorrow."

22

mik

My limbs feel heavy, as if they're filled with lead, as Noah leads me into the Bancroft estate. His arm is wrapped around my waist, holding me tightly to him. To anyone else, it would look like a loving gesture, a couple glued together through tragic loss. But I feel trapped, anchored to him when I should be running. It's a struggle to move. He had to pull me from the warm bed I've kept myself curled up in for nearly twenty-four hours after my panic attack.

I don't know why he thought it was a good idea to drag me here, why we need to keep up this charade, but I'm too tired to fight with him.

I want a drink. Alcohol to numb all my senses, my pain. I want to lose myself in it.

The estate is decorated elegantly and even though we're days away from Halloween, there's not one orange or black decoration in sight. No skulls, no roses—absolutely nothing to celebrate the holiday. No reminder of what occurred the last time a huge party was held here.

Though, this party is larger. Hundreds of people are

scattered throughout the place. Sitting in chairs, standing around high top tables and scattered throughout the formal living room, swaying to the music.

There's a pianist seated at the black grand piano, his fingers dancing across the keys, sending a soothing rhythm out into the room. "Humor me, hmm?" Noah purrs into my ear. "Dance with me."

I let him lead me. There's not a formal dance floor, just a small space where a handful of other couples are. He wraps his strong arms around my waist, pulling my hips close to his. We sway with the music, nothing fancy, and still, it takes effort for me not to lean into him, sink into his embrace.

"Mik," he whispers, his voice pleading with me. "I'm sorry. I wish it wasn't like this." He inhales deeply, then blows out a rush of air. "I wanted to keep you safe. I didn't want to hurt you like this."

Every other word that leaves his lips is about safety. The desperate pleas are grating on me. What is he keeping me safe from?

What is he lying about?

"What are you talking about?" I whisper heatedly. "What is there to keep me safe from?"

His dark eyes soften as he peers down at me. He leans in slowly, letting his lips graze my forehead. "I just want you to be happy," he murmurs.

I believe him. Grief radiates from him, but when he says the words, his voice is sturdy, and I genuinely believe him.

"There you are." Edward's voice comes between us, and Noah pulls his head away from mine. "I've been waiting for you to arrive."

Noah's grip leaves my waist, and I miss the warmth once it's gone. Miss him holding on to me.

My heart is ripped right down the middle again. The

threads that were holding it together shattered to pieces. I find myself torn between what we were and what we are. No clue what I should be doing or how I should be acting with him.

I'm thankful for Edward's interruption, something to end that conversation, end those apologies for something I don't understand.

"The man of the hour," he remarks, clapping Noah on the shoulder, beaming from ear to ear.

Noah returns the grin, except his is dimmer, less vibrant. "A free man," Noah says, his eyes directed at his father.

Only they would throw a party to celebrate murder charges being dropped after they bribed someone to do it.

I roll my eyes and try to spin away, but a hand grasps onto my elbow, dragging me back. "Mikaela." Edward smiles, and I glance down at his hand wrapped around my arm. "We need a drink to celebrate."

Edward drags us to his office, reaching for the bar cart where he keeps the more expensive bottles. "We need a good drink." He pulls the bottle of whiskey out, keeping his back to us while he pours into the crystal tumblers. Spinning around, he slides all three glasses onto the desk in front of us.

"Cheers," Noah says with a smile, clinking his glass against his fathers. They look at me expectantly, and hesitantly, I raise my glass to meet theirs. The crystal clinks against the other glasses before I bring it to my lips, letting the amber liquid slip down my throat. It burns, and I find myself coughing afterward, hating the taste.

"Will you give us a minute, Mikaela?" Edward asks, and his eyes flash between me and his son. Noah gives me a soft smile, gesturing for me to leave them, and I happily do.

Taking my glass of pure fire, I leave the two of them in Edward's office.

I find Laurel in line at the bar, with her phone glued to her hands as taps furiously on it. "Hey," she says once her eyes rise from the device. "How are you doing?"

I was thankful to have her the night before, to have a friendly face that I didn't distrust. "I'm fine," I respond. "Sorry you had to deal with that."

She shrugs, tossing a strand of dark hair over her shoulder. "Don't mention it. We all have rough patches."

I want to tell her that mine feels like more than a patch, but I stop myself. I don't want to scare off the only nice person I've talked to in a while.

"What's in that?" Laurel asks, nudging her finger at the glass of whiskey.

"Ugh," I groan. "Some fancy ass rich person whiskey. Here"—I push the glass toward her—"try it."

Laurel takes the tumbler from my hands, bringing the glass to her lips and taking a sip. As the liquid touches her lips, her green eyes go wide. "You need to throw up," she says frantically. "Where's the bathroom?"

I point down the hall, confused, but I follow her to the bathroom as she pulls on my arm, leading me down the hallway and into the room, locking the door behind us.

"Open your mouth," she demands.

I do, with a shocked look on my face. Laurel shoves two fingers into my throat, making me gag around them. It's only a few seconds before I'm spinning around, vomiting into the toilet.

When I'm done, Laurel releases my hair that she'd been holding on to and wipes my face with a paper towel.

"This is drugged," Laurel tells me, holding the glass up before pouring it down the drain.

"How do you know?" I ask.

Her eyes avoid mine for a moment before she shrugs,

trying to play off indifference. "It's not the first time I've tasted that," she tells me solemnly.

I am quiet at her admission. Putting the pieces together, I can only imagine what happened. What kind of horror she went through.

The whiskey tasted terrible, but I thought that's just how it tasted. It was the same last year when Edward poured me a glass...

My realization must show on my face because Laurel looks at me with concern. "What?" she asked. "Mikaela, what happened?"

"Edward," I whisper.

"Edward gave this to you?" She tries to lower her voice, but it still comes out high, filled with concern.

My voice won't work. I can't tell her what just happened. I'm spiraling, the truth hitting me like a ton of bricks to the chest. I thought I was drunk. For a year now, I've thought I was blackout drunk that night. I couldn't even remember what I drank. My eyes see the crystal tumbler again, knowing now that all along it wasn't me.

It was him.

He drugged me and then who knows what happened afterward. Once the drugs were in my system, there was no way I would remember a thing that happened.

Bile rises in my throat, and I feel my head whip toward the toilet again.

I can't believe it. Can't believe I was so naive, so trusting. Can't believe he would drug me right after my engagement to his son.

I can barely breathe by the time I'm done. I feel like my whole body is burning. I can feel the sweat dripping from my forehead.

"It's okay," Laurel murmurs.

But I don't believe that. And this time, I know I'm right.

I FEEL BETTER after Laurel forced me to vomit, even though I know the drugs hadn't even begun to work.

Still, I feel like some sort of weight has been lifted from my shoulders. I'm lighter, keener. Closer to the truth.

"Are you sure you're okay?" she asks me quietly as we leave the bathroom.

"I'm good," I tell her. "Thank you." It's the first appreciative remark I've given anyone since Auden's death. Thank you is a phrase of the past for me, because since that night I've been nothing but bitter and dark. But I am thankful for Laurel, more than I can even tell her. She prevented me from experiencing another hazy night of lost memories, but she also gave me an explanation, one that I'd been searching for.

With it, though, came more questions. At the top of the list, did Noah know?

I can't imagine he did. I can't fathom the idea that he allowed me to be drugged. Or allowed what happened afterward... But then I remember his hand gripped around my chin while he growled orders at me last night. I'm not sure if I even know this man anymore, or if the one I once loved is even inside that body anymore.

If he did know, my stomach turns at the thought, then he's worse than I could've even imagined. The thought that he would parade me around, knowing what happened, what his family did to me. I can't believe anyone could be so cruel.

I spare a glance at the crowd of faces around me, each of them claiming a bank account filled with more than a billion dollars. If anyone was going to be cruel, why wouldn't it be these people?

These people with money and a team of lawyers to hide their indiscretions.

"There you are." Edward finds me, linking his arm around mine and spinning us to shield Laurel from the conversation. I find myself desperately trying to turn, to find her. "I've been looking for you." Edward's smile is wide, reaching ear to ear, as he navigates me farther from Laurel, farther from the party that fills his house.

I try to yank my arm from him, but he pulls harder, pinning me to his side as he continues walking, pushing me with him.

He doesn't speak, and I spare a glance at his face, his demeanor quickly turning to ice.

Edward Bancroft has only ever been kind to me. My mind races through every encounter I've ever had with him as he leads me through the house, toward the back. Before Noah, when I was just the daughter of his employee, he shook my hand and offered kind words. With Noah, he offered me a job. He invited me to sit at his dinner table. Out to events with his friends. Sweet smiles. Kind words. Nothing ever seemed wrong.

But this is wrong.

It doesn't take a college-educated person to know that. The drug in the drink, his hold on my arm, as he leads me away from the party.

Did he do this that night too?

While my sister was dying, was I…

I can't even let the word cross my mind, can't even believe that something so terrible happened to me and I remained completely unaware.

This family, this horrible fucking family.

I yank my arm from his grasp, this time successfully, inhaling a shaky breath while I hold it against myself.

Edward's dark eyes meet mine. "What are you doing?" he growls.

"I could ask you the same thing."

His eyes wander over me and widen at the exact moment he realizes that I'm not drugged. The recognition only shows for a moment before that sinister smile rises over his lips again, spreading them thin across his face. "Mikaela," he coos my name, and the sound makes my stomach flip inside me. "I was just going to show you the theater. You said you wanted someplace quiet."

He moves toward me as he speaks the sickly sweet words. "Do you not remember?" he adds, and I feel sick all over, like I might vomit whatever scraps remain in my stomach.

"No." I hold my hand out in a feeble attempt to stop him, but he pushes it aside easily, moving in and pinning me against the wall in the hallway.

"Foolish girl," he mutters, his hot breath falling on my cheek, filling my nostrils with the scent of whiskey. "You didn't drink what I gave you?" He clicks his tongue admonishingly.

I attempt to push him away. I don't want this. His breath on my skin, his body pressed against mine. I feel the tears rise in my eyes, and I do my best to push them away, push him away.

But I can't.

I can't stop it and the idea of resigning myself to this fate feels... like death.

I would rather die.

And for a moment, I think of Auden on the edge of that cliff, what she was thinking when she stepped off the ledge.

Did she want to die too?

He pushes his lips to my face, kissing me hard and rough, but it doesn't feel the same as when Noah kisses me.

His lips are chapped, scratching at my skin. A sob lodges itself in my throat and my stomach does somersaults again.

I want to die.

The words repeat in my head. A soft mantra. And I promise myself, once this ends, I'll throw myself off that cliff too.

I see Auden's face when I close my eyes. Her hazel eyes peering back at me, her auburn hair billowing behind her. She smiles, and I feel it in my bones. Her happiness radiated from her. With that same smile, I see her look at me so clearly and say, *'Why aren't you fighting harder?'*

My eyes shoot open, and I raise my knee quickly, letting it hit him between his legs where it will hurt the most.

It works, his grip on me loosening instantly, and instead moving to cup his manhood while he calls me an obscene name. I don't wait to hear what else he has to say. I run. My heels click against the hardwood, and I'm wishing I wasn't wearing them.

Once I reach the party, where people are milling about, I kick them off, leaving them in the middle of the floor and continue running. I reach the back door, swinging it open.

My bare feet hit the decorative brick that makes out the patio before I reach the grass.

"Mikaela!" I hear someone call. Noah, I think. But I don't stop. My feet carry me, running through the grass and over rocks and sticks. I don't feel the pain anymore. Don't feel the scrapes on my soles, don't feel the burning in my legs.

I run until I hit the cliffs, until I'm gazing over the edge. In the dark, the water looks like black ink, pushing and pulling against itself. What does it feel like when you smack against it from this high up? The drop alone should kill me. At least it did for Auden. The smack against the black water and then nothing.

Silence.

I fucking crave that.

"What are you doing?" I don't hear Noah approach until he screams at me, until his arms wrap around me, pulling me backward and sending us tumbling to the ground. "What the fuck, Mik?" His words are frantic as he holds me close to his hard body.

I feel the tears slip from my eyes, the anxiety seeping out of me again. "Did you know?" I ask, unsure of the level of my voice, or if I'm even coherent enough that he can understand me.

"What are you talking about?" he asks, sitting us up but not letting go of me.

"Did you know?" I repeat. "Did you know that your dad drugged me, that he raped me?"

Shock washes over his features, and I believe it's genuine from the way his eyes widen and his grip tightens on me. "What are you talking about?" he asks again, this time lower, more concern dripping from his words.

"My drink tonight… he drugged it," I tell him. "And it was the same that night."

One hand releases me to tear through his slicked back hair, loosening it and making it unruly atop his head. "No," he muttered. "How do you know?"

"Laurel. She took a sip, and she knew, so she made me throw up. I wasn't sure…" I trail. "But then, he cornered me."

"Mik." Noah's voice is soft, and he wraps his arms around me. I accept the embrace, accept his touch. "I didn't know," he whispers, his words broken. But he believes me, I can see it. His features are soft, all the anger having drifted away.

"That's why I can't remember… he raped me." My voice is strangled, sad.

"No." Noah shakes his head. "He couldn't have."

"How? How do you know that?" I push back. He can't be sure, can't know without a doubt what happened.

"I was with you all night, Mik. I know he didn't."

"How—" I start to say.

"There you two are." Edward's voice feels like an assault to my ears. I flinch as he comes near, and Noah rises quickly, standing in front of me as a shield.

I stand too, ready to run again, to get far away from him.

"I'm sure Mikaela has told you some wild story that we both know is a lie, hmm? The girl is losing her mind. Again." He adds the last word with a tilt of his head and a sad smile, a look that says *poor girl*.

"No," Noah says sternly. "I don't think that's the case this time."

This time.

The phrase rings through my head.

Edward chuckles. "You're being silly, Son."

"No," Noah repeats. "What did you do?"

"What did *I* do?" Edward scoffs. "Your fiancée all but attacked me in the hallway, Noah. She needs help. She needs to be locked up."

I feel a strangled cry leave my lips.

I'm not crazy.

I'm *not* crazy.

Every day for a year I've felt like I was, like I was losing my mind, wracking my brain for answers to my questions and now the answers are right in front of me.

These men.

This family.

"Did you give her something?" Noah asks. "Did you drug her?" His voice is dripping with venom, the words lashing out.

Edward laughs again, the sound grating to my ears. He's

immune to the poisonous tone that leaves Noah's lips—or it doesn't bother him a bit. "Of course not. What lies is that girl spinning?"

"I don't think they're lies," Noah says, and a rush of relief blankets me. I feel less alone knowing that he believes me, that he doesn't think I'm crazy or a liar.

Edwards scoffs again, digging his hands into his pants pockets as if the accusation is amusing, a complete fabrication.

"Did you drug her?" Noah repeats, this time the words louder, angrier, like knives slashing out into the air.

But Edward is still unphased, still arrogant. "You're just looking for an excuse," he says, his dark eyes focused on me now. He takes a step forward, and I take a step back—toward the cliffs. A dangerous death march. "You just want a reason, anything to hold on to so you don't have to face what you did." His eyes sparkle with amusement, with lust, as he turns his gaze back to Noah. "Are you going to tell her, or am I?" He raises a brow as he says the words to his son.

"Shut up!" Noah shouts, the anger still there, his words still deadly, but now laced with something else, something worse. Fear.

"What is he talking about?" I ask, and I find myself backing up farther, moving away from them, a feeble attempt to escape. The heels of my feet jostle the stones I'm stepping on, and I realize I'm on the edge, only a step from going over into the inky black waves beneath me.

Edward only smiles, his teeth showing with the action. "Tell her, Son," he taunts, "Tell her, or I will."

Noah's whole body tenses, every line of his back taut, but he doesn't turn around to look at me and he doesn't say a word. The only sound coming from him is the ragged breaths he drags into his body, his chest rising with each one.

I've never seen him like this, riled up to this extent. My version of Noah has always been calm and collected, always in control. But this one? This one is feral, on edge, ready to attack.

"What is he talking about?" I ask, my voice shaky and weak, even though I try to control it. There's something happening between the three of us, something unspeakable lingering.

Edward's eyes find me again, and he takes another step closer, knowing I'm backed up as far as I can, with nowhere left to run to. That sinister laugh leaves his lips again as he looks at me. "You pushed her," he sneers, amusement in his voice. "You pushed your own sister over that ledge." He points a fat finger at my feet. "*You* killed her."

23

noah

One Year Earlier - Halloween Night

Mik is acting weird.

She has two very different drunk personalities. The flirty drunk. The one where her hands roam my body, and light kisses trail along my neck. She's happy, fun, energetic. The light of my life.

Or, the bad drunk. The one where she gets weird, sinks into her depression, lets her demons come out to play. She screams, she fights, she cries. I hate that version of her. The weak one, though I would never tell her that.

It's fitting that tonight she falls into the second category when it should be a happy night for us. She's spiraling, spinning out of control, and I can't stand the sight of it. I hate her when she's like this, and honestly, I think she hates me too.

Auden is trying to talk her down, trying to calm her, which seems unfair after she walked through the front door crying herself. Both Wilder sisters have demons hidden inside them, stuffed down so deep no one else can get through.

But I think most people do. I think we all have vaults within ourselves where we hide the things about us that we like the least. The parts of us, the memories, the things that keep us awake at night. Some do a better job of stuffing them down and hiding them than others.

I dragged them out to the patio where the two sisters are shouting at each other with tear-stained faces. Black mascara drips down both of their cheeks, marking them with the dark color. Something happened to Auden, I think, but she won't tell me. She only wants her sister. And her sister is in no state to comfort her.

And then she saw the rock on her finger, lifting her sister's hand to examine the thing before she brought her heated gaze to me. "You proposed?" she said the words accusingly. "Without her family here?"

In hindsight, I can see why that makes me an asshole, but I needed her to say yes, needed her by my side. I needed her to shield me from my own demons.

With Mik, I'm whole again, no longer the fragment of myself I am at work or with my family. I need that light in my life.

I don't give Auden the courtesy of an answer, instead I shrug.

"Why are you doing this?" Mik shouts, and I don't know if it's at Auden or the air.

She's spiraling, shouting to the wind now. She's worse than normal. How much did she drink?

"No!" she shouts, and this time, she starts running.

"Jesus," I mumble and Auden shoots daggers at me with her eyes before we both take off after her, screaming her name.

It's Auden who gets to her first. She's more practiced at

running than I am, probably from all the soccer drills. Mik led us to the cliffs, the dark waters splashing against the rock walls beneath us, and for a second, I think we're too close, but it's not the most pressing thing on my mind.

"Mikaela!" she shouts, grabbing onto her sister's shoulders. "What's going on?"

Mik lashes out, swinging her arms frantically. She's not herself, not seeing things clearly. Tears roll down her cheeks as she shouts something about them chasing her.

She pulls out of Auden's grasps and then she grabs her shoulders, holding on to her sister tightly. Before I even have a moment to inhale a breath, she spins them, pushing roughly and sending her sister flying.

"No," I scream, but the word is lodged in my throat.

I hear her body crash against the waves as I stumble to the ledge, looking over to see nothing but the dark water sprawled beneath us.

Present

"No!" Mik shouts, a finger pointed at my father, as if it could push him back or protect her.

She's too close to the edge, and memories from that night replay in my brain. I swear if Mik goes over that edge, I'll follow after her.

My father only chuckles, the sound is painful to my ears. He is amused by the whole thing. This is entertainment for him, a fucking sport.

He drugged her, I remind myself as I replay that memory again. She was so erratic, so afraid and paranoid. Now I slip all the pieces into place and all my questions get answers. She was drinking, taking edibles from Beckett, plus all the pills she takes to keep the anxiety at bay. I spare a glance at her small frame, maybe 5'5 and 130 pounds. How much can she take? How many drugs, how much liquor until she spirals out of control?

No wonder the paranoia had taken over. She was spouting nonsense, and at the time, I thought it was another symptom, another facet of depression I wasn't aware of.

How fucking stupid I must be to not have realized.

To not know what was happening right under my eyes.

How many times has my father done this? How many women has he hurt like this?

"Why?" I ask him, a slight sadness in my tone.

He shrugs. "You want to let her into this family. That means I get a taste."

Bile rises in my stomach, and I hear Mik sobbing behind me. So many thoughts are racing through my head. Why would he try to fuck my fiancée? Drug her and touch her when she didn't ask for it? My father and I have never had a good relationship, but this too far. This is sickening.

"You piece of fucking shit," I seethe, my anger back in full force.

"What are you going to do about it?" he asks, a smile stretched across his face.

"I'll tell the police, the media, everyone. I'll tell them how you like to rape young fucking girls and think you can get away with it." My tone is bitter, venom dripping from every word. I want to kill him. Violent thoughts slash through my mind. Knife. Gun. My bare hands. Anything will do.

My father chuckles, his hands tucked away in his pockets. He brings his dark gaze to me. "Good, get the police here. I have an interesting video I'd like to show them. One where she"—he lifts a finger to point at Mik—"pushes her sister over that cliff."

Fuck.

I glance up, my eyes meeting the video camera. We have them all over the property, surveillance everywhere. He's had a video this whole time, evidence that I was innocent but couldn't share for fear of her getting arrested. He told me he'd erased it.

That night, after everything happened, he was the only person I told. I trusted him like some kind of lost puppy that always runs back to its owner, despite how many times it's been kicked. I rushed Mik away, locked her in my room, hoping she'd pass out, and then I told my father everything. Exactly what Mik did.

I weave a hand through my hair. I'm out of cards. I have nothing left to play here, to protect us.

Mik is sobbing behind us, the sound gutting me, her knees on the rough dirt and stones. The truth I've been trying to protect her from is exposed now, everything out in the open. I'd been trying to save her from this pain. I didn't want her to know what she did in her drunken state. I thought I could help her, could fix her.

But I was wrong.

I couldn't protect her from this truth.

The truth always comes out, always fights its way to the surface, not caring who gets broken along the way. You can't run from the truth; it will always find a way to hunt you down.

"Fuck you," I shout.

I have nothing left to lose. Let him fire me, let him disown me. I don't care anymore.

The only thing I care about is breaking before my eyes and there's not a damn thing I can do about it.

He laughs again. "So weak, my son. How did you get this way? Was it your mother? I just don't understand," he says tauntingly. "How in the world did you become such a pathetic thing? Hmm?"

I don't know what takes over me, but I lunge at him, pushing him down to the ground and hitting him hard.

Behind us somewhere, I hear Mik screaming, crying, but I don't stop. He pushes back, rolling us over, gaining the upper hand and landing a punch to my jaw. He's too big, too slow, and I roll him back over.

"Stop!" I hear Mik shout, but everything in my line of vision is shielded. I'm surrounded by darkness, just me and him, and I can't stop. I can't stop fighting him, and I don't care about the consequences.

"Stop!" she shouts again, her words pleading with me, but I ignore her, the red lining my vision too strong, too overpowering. I want to hurt him, to make him suffer the way I have, the way Mik has.

I roll one more time, but this time, it's different. This time, I realize I roll him over the cliff. I feel Mik grab on to my ankle, and as the red haze recedes, I realize that my hands around my father's arms are the only thing holding him above that dark water.

The only thing keeping him alive.

Somehow, I'm still on the ground, just my chest hanging over the edge and Mik holding on to my legs with every ounce of strength she has, fearing me falling over the edge as well.

I look down at him, if only for a second, and find his dark eyes meeting mine.

It's fitting, I think.

How the tables have turned, the power dynamic flipped around. For a moment, I think, *he's still my father*. But just as quick, an image of his hands on Mik's body infiltrates my mind. Him drugging her, touching her, all without her ever knowing.

I let go, let him drop. There's a sad scream as he falls,

bouncing off the rock walls, and the only thing I can think is... *who's pathetic now?*

MIK IS CLINGING TO ME. Tears rush from her eyes, sobs heaving from her chest. Her face is a mess of black mascara, and she holds me, holds me for the first time in a long time.

I wrap my arms around her and catch my breath, suddenly aware of how much my chest aches.

We stay there for a while like that. Just breathing heavily, my father's body somewhere beneath us in the black ink of the water.

I ONLY TELL David the truth. And we call the police together, having them head out to this house for the second time in a year while we usher people out of the party.

While we wait for cops, I head to the security room. I want to clear two tapes.

One from tonight, and one from a year ago.

The security room is hidden on the first floor in the far back, locked with a thumbprint scanner that only my father, mother, and I can access. I press my thumb to the smooth surface, letting the door click to let me in.

But the room is black, every monitor off, every recording device down for the night. It's weird, because my father never turns the security system off. We have far too many valuables to risk any of them going missing or anyone sneaking onto the property.

I boot up the system, letting the computer roar to life. Once it's on again, I scroll through the history, finding

October 31st of last year. Nothing after six PM, nothing but black screens, not a single recording.

An ache hits my chest as I remember the drugged drink he gave Mik. How she thinks he gave her one that night too...

How many other nights are blank?

How many girls have fallen victim to my father?

Every last doubt I had about letting him go suddenly vanish.

WHEN THE POLICE FINALLY ARRIVE, everyone else is gone. I do most of the talking, a shaking Mik sitting beside me, wrapped in a blanket, and David on the other side. My mother sits on one of her custom-made chairs, a tissue glued to her hand as she dabs at the slow falling tears.

I push all my emotions aside while I take control of the situation. I can't feel sorry for myself, for Mik. Not yet. Not until I know we're safe.

I tell them what happened, but not without a twist.

I tell them how Mik had confronted my father, how he had drugged her drink, and when she called him on it, he admitted to everything. He told her how he took Auden out to the cliffs that night, and when she wouldn't do what he wanted, he pushed her over the edge.

Then I tell them how grief stricken he was, how bad he felt about the ordeal.

I tell them that I watched him walk off that ledge, his sorrow finally consuming him.

My mother doesn't question our story, and I wonder for a brief moment if she knows I'm a liar, or if she's always known what my father was capable of. Stood by his side while he drugged and manipulated young girls. Did she ever love him? Does she even care that he's dead?

Mik, the only witness to my crime, doesn't dispute my story a bit. Only nodding in agreement while she wraps her blanket tighter around her.

We share something now, the bond of accidentally killing someone, and we both want to bury those memories, stuff them down so deep until they disappear.

I can already feel the bruises rising on my skin. I know it must be obvious that I was in a fight.

But nobody questions our story.

24

mik

"There's one more thing I need to know," I tell Noah as we approach the small bungalow house in my old neighborhood.

He stuffs his palms into the pockets of his fitted black jeans. "Are you sure?" he questions, one brow lifted. "You don't think you've gotten enough truth for one lifetime?"

I've probably had more than enough, but I still need to know this one last thing. "One more thing," I assure him, tossing him a soft smile.

He wants to bury this night behind us, and I can't say I blame him. We've spent a year of our lives reliving one night. Chasing down all of the secrets and searching for justice. It's broken us in ways I don't think we'll ever recover from.

He still has a black eye and some yellowing bruises along his abdomen. We buried his father with a small ceremony. Mariam knew immediately that we had lied. She knew something else had gone down, but she didn't want to hear the words from our lips. She told Noah she knew about the cameras… why they were off. The two shared an understanding look and then pushed it behind them, never to be spoken of again.

We cling to each other, praying that this alone is enough, that we can carry each other through it. I think the worst part is over now. Now we just need to pick up all the shattered pieces and try to create something new.

We'll do it with her in mind.

We've both lost something now, a part of ourselves going over that cliff that night with Edward. The truth had found me, having scratched its way out. For a while I thought if I knew what happened I would suddenly feel better, but that's not how it works.

I feel worse.

But I understand why he hid it from me, why he tried to protect me, even if in the end, it didn't work.

I knock on the dark wooden door of the old house. Noah lifts his sunglasses from his head and tucks them neatly into the pocket of his leather jacket.

My skin buzzes as we wait. I feel like the final puzzle piece is just on the other side of this door.

"Hello?" It's Kelly who answers, Auden's best friend. Tight jeans hug her legs, and she wears a loose peasant top. Her eyes grow wide when she sees me.

"Hi," I say with a tight smile. "Can we come in?"

She is silent as she gestures for us to enter. She's eighteen now, and she looks more mature than the last time I saw her. She's a senior in high school, and I wonder what Auden would have looked like at eighteen, as a senior. I wonder if she would have changed, who she would have loved? She'll forever live inside me as a seventeen-year-old, never aging, never growing. She'll never get to be like Kelly.

"I just have one question," I say as we sit down on the couch across from Kelly.

I pull out the photocopy of the text messages Auden sent

me, handing it over to her. "These are all the messages my sister sent the night she died. What happened at that party, Kelly? Why was she so upset?"

Kelly chews on a nail while she reads through the messages; Auden's pleas for me to help her. When she lifts her gaze, her eyes are lined with tears that are ready to fall.

"I'm sorry," Kelly whispers, the first tear dropping.

Noah shifts on the couch next to me, leaning forward with interest. He thought this was silly, begged me to let this one go, that it was probably nothing.

He admitted to deleting the text messages, figuring we would never know what led my sister to his parents' house that night. He finally admitted this transgression in the emptiness of his house, with the two of us cuddled in front of the fireplace, trying to come to terms with our truths. He wanted to protect me, protect me from the feelings that coursed through my body. Regret, pain, sadness.

Auden had been crying when she arrived at his parents' house, but nobody knew why.

The sadness in Kelly's eyes tells me that she might be the only one who knows.

"I didn't tell your parents," she says quickly. "I didn't want them to be mad, and she was already gone, ya know? What good would it have done?"

"Kelly," I say her name slowly. "Tell me what happened."

"Auden would be…" She trails off. "Embarrassed."

"I know she was planning to have sex that night. Did something happen with a boy?"

Her eyes shift when I tell her what I know, and she nods slowly. "Yeah, it was Carson. They went upstairs and then she came back down really quick after, and she was crying. I asked her what was wrong and she…" Kelly slows, taking a deep breath before she continues. "She said he was going too fast, and it hurt, and she asked him to stop, but he wouldn't. So she went to run away, I guess, and he got angry."

I feel another piece of my heart break, falling and shattering. I wish I was there for her. I wish I could have told her that guys like that suck. That I would chase them down and kill them all for her.

That she deserves better.

Even with the pain, I needed to know, to hear this.

"And then she left," Kelly finishes. "She called an Uber, and she left." Kelly is crying now, tears streaming down her cheeks. "I didn't want to upset anyone anymore, so I just didn't say anything."

"It's okay," I tell her, wrapping her in a hug. "You were just trying to be a good friend."

Kelly shakes her head, spewing her own regrets. Wishing she would have chased after Auden or done something.

I tell her not to think like that.

You can't live in the past, can't let the demons hunt you down.

When I step out of the bungalow later, I feel different.

Complete, in a weird way. Like I solved a puzzle, and now I have one less thing holding me down, one less weight on my chest.

There's still so much pain. It swallows me whole some nights, but I steal a glance over at Noah. The engagement ring still sits on my finger, waiting for the wedding band to complete the set.

I'm not fixed, not even close, and neither is he. I still wake with nightmares, visions of things I never want to remember again.

But right now, I feel a shift. I think I can feel her near me, telling me it's okay. Auden was always more forgiving than me. For being younger, she was kinder, more gracious. I think she would tell me to move on, to live my life to the fullest. For both of us.

I wonder if Auden is happy, if she can rest peacefully, knowing that I know now.

EPILOGUE

noah

Five Years Later

We still celebrate Halloween. Only now, we do it far from the lives we left behind. California was the fresh start we both needed. Leaving everyone behind and moving forward, just the two of us.

It wasn't hard for me to find a leadership position at a Silicon Valley tech company and Mik finished her business degree virtually. We sold my shares of my father's company. After his death, running his company felt more like a death sentence than an accomplishment. And a fresh start was needed for both of us.

The extra money made it unnecessary for Mik to work, not that she would have needed to anyway. She decided to volunteer instead, and I couldn't deny the happiness it brought her. She finally found a passion, something she felt strongly about.

She sits on the board of a local mental health organization, one that works to pair volunteers with kids and adults suffering from mental illness. Mik knows every kid in the place, can tell you their whole history and diagnosis. She's sat with each of them, letting them talk her ear off about their problems. I give her credit; she's patient and kind and gives her whole self to each patient.

And it warms my heart to watch her live, to care about something bigger than herself.

She's no longer the scared and fragile woman she was the year after Auden's death. I didn't believe that the truth could set her free. I was sure that it would bury her, haunt her every nightmare. But then again, I didn't know what my father had done to her either.

We don't talk about our secret. Some things you just don't speak about. We left it buried in Maryland under six feet of dirt. As far as anyone knows, my father was the one who killed Auden, and we're just happy that the truth was revealed before his death.

I take a sip of my gin as I watch her. She's organizing full-sized candy bars, so they sit aesthetically in the black caldron she bought. When she's done, she looks up at me with a cheesy grin. "What do you think?"

"I love it," I tell her. I don't really give a fuck how the candy looks. Truly, I didn't even want to give out candy. I wanted to lock the doors and take her upstairs and fuck her until she's filled with my cum.

But Halloween is important to her. So I watch for hours as she opens the door and coos over the dressed up children. Princesses, superheroes, ghosts, and pumpkins. She gets equally excited for each one as she extends her cauldron and lets the kids pick their poison.

I can't lie, though. I like watching her like this, happy and in her element. The way she oohs and ahhs over each child makes me want to see her with her own, something we've been putting off longer and longer.

Children are a commitment we're afraid of. After all

we've done and witnessed, who's to say if our child would be *okay* or *normal?* What if we fuck it up just like us?

And if I have these fears, I can only imagine the spiral of thoughts swimming through Mik's head. So we put it off, again and again.

I like the idea of little Miks, but I can also see a lifetime of just the two of us.

When it gets dark, and the trick or treaters are all gone, Mik closes the door with a sigh and sets her nearly empty cauldron down.

"Come here." I gesture for her to sit on my lap. She crosses the living room with a smile on her face until she gets to me in my chair. Her round ass comes down on my lap and her shoulder presses against my chest.

"Hi," she whispers, tucking her head into the crook of my neck.

"Hi," I mimic, leaning in so I can place a soft kiss on her lips. "You look amazing," I tell her. She's wearing a goofy sweatshirt with pumpkins, ghosts, and black cats, paired with tight black shorts. She doesn't dress up anymore.

Her head tilts back when she laughs, and her blonde hair falls over her shoulder. "Thank you. So do you." Her finger clasps onto the lapels of my suit jacket.

I want her. I always want her. Through everything we've been through, my need for her has never wavered. I wrap my fingers around the back of her head, pulling her toward me until her lips touch mine. Deepening the kiss, I move my hands to her waist and shift her until she's straddling me. Her eyes pop open and there's excitement lingering in the pools of green while she watches me, waiting for the next move.

"Tell me what you want, baby girl." I smile wickedly.

"Whatever you want," she replies, so submissively, always trying to make me happy.

"Uh-uh," I chide. "Answer me,"

She tugs her bottom lip between her teeth while she thinks. "You," she answers, her voice low and sweet. "Inside me..." There's a slight curve to her lips as she looks up at me.

I press another kiss to her temple. "That I can do. First, on your knees."

She complies so quickly, so sweetly. Hopping from my lap and lowering to her knees in front of me. I stand from my chair, stripping off my blazer while her fingers undo my belt buckle.

With a devilish grin, Mik lowers my slacks and boxers to my ankles until I can step out of them. She licks her lips when her eyes line up with my cock and the sight alone is enough to send a shudder down my spine.

"Suck," I demand, and she wastes no time.

She starts with my balls, running the tip of her tongue over them in slow, teasing circles. I want to tell her to cut the shit, but the feeling is intoxicating. She moves her tongue from my balls all the way up to the tip of my cock, licking every inch along the way.

When she reaches the top, her eyes flick up to mine. There's a sparkle there when she sees how I'm watching her. She knows me as well as I know her. All of my likes, dislikes, quirks, she knows them like the back of her hand.

She licks her lips before she takes in my entire length, swallowing me until the tip hits the back of her throat. I groan, and the sound makes her moan while she swallows my cock. Her mouth feels like fucking *heaven*.

Pulling back up, she sucks in a breath before she begins to work, bobbing her head up and down on my cock while her saliva lubes it up. She's messy, and at one point, she brings her hand into the mix, twisting it as she continues her motions.

It feels like pure ecstasy, but this isn't how I want to come tonight.

"Stop." I pull back from her, breathless. She smiles up at me, looking victorious. It's a game between us, one where she tries to break my control. She never wins, but she prides herself on getting close.

I want to drag her upstairs and fuck her in our bed, but I can't wait that long. I need her now.

"Strip," I tell her.

She does. Standing up and ridding herself of her clothes, piece by piece. The shorts and the sweatshirt fall to the floor, followed by a simple pair of black panties and a black bra.

"Bend over the side of the couch," I order.

She listens immediately, rising to her feet and moving to the edge of the couch. She bends over the edge and flips her blonde hair over her shoulder so she can look back at me.

I like the sight of her like this, naked and waiting for me.

I run my palms over the curves of her ass, the smooth skin on display, before bringing my fingers to her pussy. She's already soaked, and I groan with the realization. "Did sucking my cock get you wet, baby girl?"

I can see the blush rise on her cheeks, heating her with a pretty pink.

"Nothing to be ashamed of, baby. I think it's hot as fuck that it makes you horny."

"Noah," she whines, wiggling her ass. "Please, fuck me already."

I land a palm on her ass cheek, and she yelps with the surprise pain. "I'll fuck you when I'm ready, baby."

I use my fingers first, dragging her wetness down to her clit and rubbing slow circles around it. She needs to come first. It's always better for her if she gets one orgasm in. She starts to pant when I pick up speed, and when I add an extra digit to her sex, she starts to grind on it, trying her best to fuck herself.

"Stay still, Mik," I order. "Take what I give you."

Like a good girl, she does. Her fingers clench onto the couch cushion as I make her come, and when she falls over the edge, she screams out my name.

Before she has a chance to catch her breath, I fuck her. Thrusting my length into her. Her fingers grip onto the cushion again, regretting letting go for that brief second.

I fuck her until she screams out my name like a god. And when she falls over the edge a second time, I follow her over that cliff, filling her with my cum.

Afterwards, I scoop her up in my arms and carry her upstairs to the master bathroom. She's hazy and calm and she looks at me with such adoration in her eyes. These are the moments I live for. The harmonious minutes where everything else has drifted away and all that is left is just us. The people we believe ourselves to be. The past and the future are gone. Nonexistent. And we don't have to remember the things we've done to be together.

It's just us.

Always just us.

THANK YOU FOR READING SHATTERED! If you love dark and kinky romance, I have more books for you!

Check out Alliance, a mafia forbidden romance, now!

A sinner met a saint,
Two worlds collided,
And everything burned.

Lana

I've done everything right.
Playing the part of the demure *famiglia* daughter,
And hiding my pain beneath makeup and pretty dresses.
But marrying a man ten years my senior?
Whose words cut like knives,
And lips taste like poison.
This is the one thing I can't do.

Naz
I've done nothing right.
I'm not a virtuous man,
I balance on the line between light and dark.
My past is littered with sins,
Each of them is haunting me.
I'm not worthy of the angel with long hair and hazel eyes.
And yet, I'd burn the city to the ground to hold her in my arms.

What's a sinner to do?

ACKNOWLEDGMENTS

I'm not sure where to start here. When I started writing, I did so in private, hiding it from everyone like a dirty secret. Now, however long later, I have a whole crew. So many people have supported me in this writing ad- venture, more than I ever thought would. That support means the world to me.

I can honestly say this book wouldn't be here if it wasn't for Thalia and my husband, Jake. This book was different, it felt weird and foreign the entire time I wrote it. I kept second guessing if it was a love story, honestly, I still do, but the two of you were there the entire way pushing me forward.

Thalia (aka @thalsettgrace and @authorthaliasanchez), you are the best alpha reader, beta reader, hype woman, author friend, and fellow dog mom that I could ever ask for. You read this book when it was only a few rough chapters and I had no idea what the story was, but I knew there were people with a lot of pain. You cheered me on every step of the way, asking questions, and loving the characters. I am so effing thankful to have you in my life.

My babe, AKA the husband, just when I thought you had maximized your supportiveness, you upped the game. I think loving me while I'm writing is probably really hard. I stop thinking about anything that is not the book and it becomes the only thing I can talk about. Thank you for sitting at the dining room table for hours talking about this plot with me, for listening to me talk about this book nonstop, and for letting me hide in my office for two months. Thank you for sticking with me through all of my crazy. I know you think this is a really cool murder mystery and not a sex book, and I love that about you.

Anna Widzisz, my partner in crime and fellow mafia babe. I am so thankful this crazy world brought us together. You have been such a gem in my life, and I will never be able to thank you enough listening to me talk about my books, for supporting them, and for always being there for me. Once this pandemic is over, we are traveling together, I wrote it in this book so now it's real.

To the ladies of Books & Moods: Julie, Val, and Mary – thank you for everything. The cover of this book is gorgeous, as soon as I saw it, I knew it was the perfect fit for Mik. Val, thank you for all the beautiful graphics you created for these two. I look at them almost every day... Julie, thank you for all your support and responses to my 50,000 messages a day. I hope I'm not your worst client, lol. And Mary, thank you for your support as well! For the edits and for sending me all the book recommendations for my post writing break.

Big thank you to all the bloggers, reviewers, and bookstagramers who have supported me along this journey. I can't thank you enough for taking the time to read my books and talk about them.

Last, but not least, thank you, yes you. My reader. Whether you loved or hated this book, thank you for picking it up and giving my work a chance. Writing has always been the dream for me so to think that anyone is reading this is absolutely amazing. So, thank you!

ALSO BY NATALIA LOUROSE

The Sinners of New Orleans

Alliance

Deception

Obsession (Coming Fall 2022)

Birthright (Coming Winter 2022)

The Delgado Trilogy

Gio

Gemma

Gian

ABOUT THE AUTHOR

Natalia Lourose writes angsty romance about broken people figuring out life and finding love along the way. Television and far too much smut as a teenager left her obsessed with dark-haired bad boys who are moody and wear leather jackets. Tucked away in her writing nook with a dog at her feet, two cats on her keyboard, and husband yelling at the computer – she is always writing something, or trying to.

Printed in Great Britain
by Amazon